MERRY MARY

Malinda Martin

Other Books by Malinda Martin

Matchmaking Angels Series

Shamrocks & Matchmaking Angels
Cinnamon Tea & Matchmaking Angels
Croissants & Matchmaking Angels

Castle Clubhouse Romance Series

The Course of True Love
All's Fair in Love and Fame
The Best Laid Plans
The Write One
Where There's Smoke
Down the Romance Hole
Writing Exes
No Business Like Romance Business

Christmas in Charity Series

Christmas Grace
Comfort and Joy
Merry Mary
Carol of the Bells
Faith, Hope, & Mistletoe
Good Tidings

Beaumont Family Series

Heartthrob

Heart And Soul
Heart Attack
Heartbreak

The Biggest Part of Me

Christmas Dad

Forgetting Christmas

Sleep In Heavenly Peace Inn Series

Sleep In Heavenly Peace Inn
Sleep In Heavenly Peace Inn Two
Sleep In Heavenly Peace Inn Three

The Midnight Kiss Series

The Midnight Kiss
The Midnight Dance
The Midnight Bride

Tennessee Waltz

Tennessee Shuffle

For more information on sweet romance by
Malinda Martin, go to www.malindamartin.com.

Your free books are waiting!

Do you enjoy sweet romance, holiday stories, Christian Fiction?

You can get three stories for free. That's right, three! It's a special gift to you for signing up for Malinda Martin's monthly newsletter.

To get your free books, go to <u>www.malindamartin.com</u>. You'll also receive information on other sweet romance and Christian fiction novels.

Dedicated to the memory of
John Wayne and Maureen O'Hara,
one of my favorite movie couples
and the inspiration
for the characters of Frank and Merrilyn Swenson.

"Have yourself a merry little Christmas . . ."

Chapter One

Small towns are the backbone of America, an important aspect of the fabric of our society. A place where real people deal with real life.

Mary Swenson would have given her last dollar to be hundreds of miles from this particular one—Charity, Florida.

"And I say that an elf mud wrestling competition would entertain one and all for the Christmas season," a homeowner was suggesting at the monthly town meeting.

"Yeah, Carter. It'd be just clean ol' fun, huh?" another man replied to which the audience chuckled and murmured his or her own opinion.

"All right, folks. We really need to get on with the meeting." Mayor Howard Scott's voice rose to get everyone's attention.

Mary pinched between her eyes to prevent the headache that was brewing.

Charity had become a travel destination for the holidays, due in large part by the phenomenal success of the book *Christmas In America*, the bestseller by famous photographer Stuart "Mac" McCrae, the co-owner of the local diner. The pretty main street of the town was featured on the cover, a magical picture that had captured the hearts of millions.

The only problem was that the little town was trying to think of something to do with all the sightseers when they came.

"I think, Mr. Carter, that the mud wrestling should be put on the list of 'maybes' for now," the mayor said.

Yes. Like maybe on the eve of never, Mary thought.

Mayor Scott had asked the attendees to write suggestions on slips of paper and as he read out each, nothing seemed to fit the task of showcasing the essence of Charity. Mary looked at her watch wondering how much longer the meeting would last before Howard decided to let the town council handle the situation.

"The next suggestion is . . ." Howard pulled out another slip of paper. "Have a Santa look-a-like contest."

Really? Really?

The excited crowd broke out in loud discussion of why this would or would not work.

Howard raised his voice and said, "Colin, I believe this was yours. Care to elaborate?"

The town handyman looked around and then stood. "Yeah. I just think we could have the event on Main Street and invite men of all ages to show us their best Santa costume and 'ho, ho, ho.' I think everyone would get a real kick out of it."

"And what about the children, Colin." Everyone turned to see the speaker, Harriet Wingate, wife of the local bank president and resident busybody. "Don't you think it would traumatize the children to see all those Santa's? Do we really want to scar the youth of America any more than they already are?"

Harriet always was a little dramatic.

"Let's ask an expert," Harriet continued. "Carol Baker is one of our kindergarten teachers. Miss Baker, what do you think?"

Mary winced. Carol was a quiet, unassuming teacher. The last thing she'd want was to be the center of attention at a town meeting.

"Oh, I . . . ah, I don't know. I suppose it would be important . . . um, how the event was handled."

Mary gave the woman an encouraging smile. "Good job," she whispered.

"You say something, Mary?"

She turned to the man sitting next to her. Brad Moore. Some people would call him her boyfriend. Well, yes, they had been going out fairly often for the past six months, but she was hardly infatuated. Brad blinked his big brown eyes behind his black-rimmed glasses as he glanced at her. He was a tall, solid, good-natured . . . scientist. That was the best way to describe him. Even now, in the middle of a meeting about their community he was hunched over a report he was proofing to be published in the next edition of *Science Today*. Yes, she was impressed, even if she didn't know what the heck the report was about.

Not wanting to explain the situation with Carol, she whispered, "It's nothing. Just go back to your report."

"Another interesting idea," Howard said diplomatically. "Another definite maybe." He pulled out another idea. "Hmm. Interesting. The suggestion here is to hold a Christmas sing-a-long at Hal's Place."

"What?"

Mary turned to see her good friend Grace McCrae, co-owner of the local diner, standing with hands on her hips, incredulity on her face.

"You have got to be kidding. There is no way we can accommodate all the tourists that come to Charity for the season at one time for a big event like that. Not going to happen."

Another voice in the crowd sounded. "That don't sound like such a good idea. It's going to push out the regulars and we don't want that, right Daddy?" The man speaking, Little Jed, the fiftyish son of the elder Big Jed, was adamant. He looked over at his father who sat with his arms folded across his chest napping.

The chatter and murmurs started again. Mary saw her father make his way into the room and down her row, giving her a sheepish grin. "Did I miss anything?"

Mary snorted. "The next time you want me to attend a town meeting for you, I'm going to be busy. Just saying." She dusted off a piece of lint from his suit jacket and then kissed his cheek, giving him a grin.

Frank Swenson chuckled as he settled in his chair and put his arm around his daughter. Then noticed the man on the other side of her. "Hello,

Brad," he said quietly. Brad grunted, his eyes never leaving his papers.

"I picked up a new bottle of vitamins, Dad. You were running low. And I scheduled a massage at the club for you, Saturday at one o'clock." When Frank groaned, she said, "No complaining. You've been working too hard lately and I don't like how exhausted you look." She gave him another kiss and added, "I want you to be around for a long time. So you'll go for the massage?"

His lopsided grin and deep sigh had Mary smiling. He'd go.

Mary loved her father. He had and would always be her knight in shining armor, a handsome prince, and all those euphemisms that women attribute to the perfect man. He was slim, but not skinny. Handsome, but not overly so. Mary simply adored him.

She'd never been able to understand why her mother didn't.

"Could we please get back to the meeting, folks?" Mayor Scott said without much success.

Mary wondered why he didn't just end the thing. Obviously they weren't going to make any progress tonight. It was futile to try to reach a consensus with these people. Especially since it was doubtful that there would be one decent idea. Couldn't Mayor Scott see that?

These aren't the ideas you're looking for, she thought. But apparently the mayor ignored the Jedi mind trick that Mary was trying to use on him, because he reached into the hat for another suggestion. Above the continued noise from the crowd, he said, "Ah, here's an interesting one."

He looked straight at Mary and said, "Mary Swenson has suggested that we have a Christmas Eve parade through downtown Charity."

As if the volume of a television was muted, everyone now turned to look at Mary. She felt her face heat with the attention. It had been just a spur of the moment idea, something to write down. She hadn't expected anyone to actually consider it.

"Mary. Tell us about this parade idea."

The room was silent. Except for Big Jed's gentle snoring.

She looked at the mayor. Then her father. Then all around her. Even Brad was waiting for her response. Great, just great. She'd have to think of something fast.

She cleared her throat and said, "Well, I just thought that . . . we have a parade on the Fourth of July and everyone seems to like it. Why not do the same for Christmas?"

Mayor Scott's eyes gazed out, his mind working on the idea. "Yes, I see. It would get the whole community involved. Could be a big event outdoors to accommodate the crowds." He thought for another second and then glanced around. "And what do the citizens of Charity think?"

"I love the idea!" Harriet said.

"Logistics would be easy enough to do," Colin added.

"Me and Daddy are all for it!" Little Jed exclaimed raising his sleeping father's hand with his.

"Great," the mayor said. "All in favor of a Christmas Eve parade with Mary Swenson in charge give me a big 'aye.'"

"What? No! I mean nay! I didn't mean to . . ."

But Mary knew it was too late as the room filled with a robust shout of "Aye." She was now in charge of the Charity Christmas Eve Parade.

She was numb as people came by to congratulate her on her brilliant idea and wishing her much success. Sure. And where would those people be when she was scrounging around at the last minute to put the darn thing together. She could kick herself.

Once most everyone was gone, her father grinned and put an arm around her shoulders. "There now, Mary. It'll be okay. The thing to do is to delegate. Get others to do the work."

Easy for one of the most successful land developers in Central Florida. She was a lowly real estate agent without hordes of people at her beck and call.

A thought struck and she gasped. "Our vacation, Dad! Bermuda! What are we going to do?"

"Now honey," he said as he guided her out of Town Hall. "We'll take a later flight. How about you plan the parade for Christmas Eve morning and then we get a flight out that afternoon? Come on, now," he said rubbing her shoulder. "We'll work it out."

She let her head drop onto the strong shoulder that she loved. "I hope so," she sighed as they walked away.

Nothing seemed to be going right. There were glitches in several of the real estate deals she was putting together. The initial planning for the parade was going slowly. And she had a weird sense of trouble approaching.

Added to that, her father had been in a terrible disposition lately. It was as if he too had the feeling of impending doom.

That's why Mary was hiding out at Hal's Place, the little diner in downtown Charity, having a cup of coffee with her good friend Grace. But it wasn't helping. Grace was currently complaining about her own problems, primarily her husband's busy schedule.

Mary sighed. Even the idealistic marriage of Grace and Mac had problems.

Marriage. Why did men and women go through the trouble of committing their lives to each other when the whole concept was unrealistic? Hadn't her own parents' marriage shown her that?

She'd grown up the loved, only child of Frank and Merrilyn Swenson. She'd thought her parents had a good marriage—loving companionship, only occasional disagreements, affectionate kisses.

Then five years ago while she was at college at Columbia University in New York City, her mother showed up and said she'd moved down the street. Just like that. No explanations. No excuses. No reasons. Just snap, "I'm living here now. Let's have tea."

It had soured her on the idea of marriage, that's for sure. She didn't need a therapist to tell her that's why she dated a man that she had absolutely no intention of uniting with in holy matrimony.

Still, she wondered why her parents had never gotten a divorce. For five years they had lived separately, Merrilyn in New York and Frank in Charity.

Mary would never admit that it still hurt to think about it.

She stirred her coffee and pretended to be sympathetic to Grace's plight of her absentee husband. *Just be glad you don't have kids, Grace.*

"So, what do you think? Mary?"

Mary's head jerked up. Grace was apparently waiting for an answer to her question. Embarrassed to be caught daydreaming, Mary said, "Sorry. What was that?"

Grace frowned. "Are you okay? It's not like you to be so distracted."

"I guess I've just got a lot on my mind just now."

Grace reached over and covered Mary's hand with her own. "Yeah. The town sorta railroaded you into heading up the parade. Although it was a very good idea."

Mary smirked.

"I'm sure everyone will help you. Don't try to do this on your own."

"Dad and I had planned to travel to Bermuda to spend the holidays."

"That's right. Your annual Christmas trip." Grace took a sip of coffee and then carefully said, "You spending New Years in New York with your mom?"

"Mmm." Mary sipped her coffee. "Christmas with Dad. New Years with Mom. Happy holidays," she said sarcastically.

Grace sighed. "I really hate to see you down." Patting her hand, she added, "What you need is a little Christmas spirit."

Mary chuckled. "This from the woman that used to forbid any decorations within twenty feet of Hal's Place. My, how you've changed in a few short years."

A satisfied smile covered Grace's face as she took another sip. Mary was happy for the transformation in Grace. Before Grace would comment, Mary said, "And now you put up so many lights I don't know how you're not cited by the electric company."

Now Grace laughed. "I know, we go a little overboard. I'm just making up for lost time."

"Grace, could you check this order? Oh, hi Mary," a petite, dark-haired waitress said, approaching their booth.

"Hi, Joy. How's the family?"

"*Magnifique*," she answered in her gentle French accent.

Then as Grace scowled, Mary and Joy began a rapid conversation in French. "Hey," Grace said, rapping the table to get their attention. "English only. Have a heart, will you?"

Joy smiled warmly at Mary. "But of course. I was merely inviting Mary over for dinner. If I offended, I am sorry."

Grace smirked as the doors of the diner opened admitting Hal's Place regulars Big Jed and Little Jed.

"Joy, could you get us coffee?" Both men took a seat at the counter, their cheeks a rosy red, their eyes glowing with excitement.

"So, what's going on, fellas?" Grace asked, everyone knowing that the two were the best in town at relaying the latest gossip.

Joy set down waters along with the coffee. Little Jed took a sip of water allowing his father to speak. "Well, you'll just never guess what we seen. I swear you'd think it was the circus coming to town."

All three women looked at the Jeds waiting for an explanation. But Big Jed was enjoying the attention too much, deciding he'd like to drag the story out.

"Could have been a VIP or a politician. Maybe even a movie actor. Closest thing I remember to this was when that musician, one of them Beatles, got lost and he and his band ended up in Charity." Big Jed laughed. "Didn't know what he was getting into when that group of women in their purple hats saw him and started screaming." Little Jed joined in the laughter.

Everyone loved the Jeds but enough was enough.

"Okay, we get it. Now would you please tell us exactly what you saw?" Grace said.

"Yes," Mary agreed. "What did you see?"

"Oh, well we was walking across the bridge over on the avenue and we seen this caravan heading in. Several of them moving trucks. But the car in the front was something else. It was some kind of fancy foreign convertible, bright red, shiny just like a ripe apple."

Little Jed took over the story. "Driving the car was a woman wearing these big black sunglasses and her hair in some kind of bright red scarf."

"Yeah, a long scarf that was blowing in the wind," Big Jed added.

At that moment, the hair on the back of Mary's neck stood straight up. She felt the blood drain from her face and her throat dried up.

That impending doom had just arrived.

Chapter Two

Grace listened with interest as Little Jed continued.

"And next to the lady was some man duded up in a suit looking like he just ate some of Loretta's sour pickles."

"I heard that," came the voice of the offended cook from the kitchen.

"Wow." Grace said, leaning back in her seat. "That's certainly . . . Mary? Are you okay?"

Mary stared at the two men. "Are you sure about all that?"

"As sure as I'm sitting here, pretty Mary, that's what we saw. The convoy headed toward them big houses on the north end of town. Right where you—hey! Where you going?"

But the door of the diner was already closing as Mary ran out. Leaving everyone in the diner perplexed.

Grace got up and took her coffee cup back to the kitchen as Big Jed and Little Jed continued to chat with Joy. She wondered about her friend. Something was going on and she'd go crazy until she found out. A good thing since it would give her something to worry about instead of Mac's crazy schedule.

"I'm making an order this afternoon, Sal. Loretta. How are supplies holding out?" She halfway listened as she put her mug in the dishwasher.

Why couldn't she stop thinking about Mac having to be gone for business? His photographs and books were selling better than ever, why did that mean he had to be gone more? It was the holiday season and she wanted to be with her husband, not sharing the news of a Charity Christmas over the phone.

It had been so romantic when they'd fallen in love with Christmas carols playing around them. Maybe the holidays reminded her of that.

But she wasn't a foolish young girl believing she was in a fairy tale. This was real life and Mac had to earn a living doing what he loved. She couldn't, wouldn't try to take that away from him.

She'd just have to get through it and support her husband as a good wife should.

But she didn't have to like it.

Mary was numb. It couldn't be. By the time she made it to the estate home of her father, the trucks had started unloading. Mary slammed the brakes of her baby blue BMW sedan and sat there gaping. *It can't be.*

She pulled to the edge of the curb, far away from the trucks so that they wouldn't hit her car when they left, hopefully in the next few minutes.

The movers were carrying out suitcase after suitcase (made of expensive Italian leather) along with small appliances, upholstered furniture, linens, towels, and accessories—everything a person would want to equip a home. A home in the finest penthouse of Manhattan, that is.

Mary looked around looking for the person in charge. Finding a heavy set, older man with thinning hair holding a clipboard and a pen, she walked over. "Excuse me. I think there's been a big misunderstanding here. Would you please stop your men for a moment?"

The man didn't even look up from his board. "Can't. Busy. We've got to get this job done and head back up to Jacksonville."

Frustrated, Mary said, "Listen, fella, this is my house you're putting all this junk into and if you don't stop this instant you're going to find yourself talking to the police."

Apparently that got the man's attention. He looked up at her and whistled between his fingers, causing his men to stop where they were.

Mary thought it an impressive trick but concealed her amazement and said, "Would you please tell me where the woman is who ordered your services?"

His head jerked towards the open front door.

Mary looked at the house with a great deal of trepidation. More than anything she wanted to get back in her car and head out of town, maybe drop the parade in someone else's lap and head to

Bermuda early. But she wouldn't leave without her dad.

Oh, her poor dad.

Mary straightened the navy blue jacket she wore over the matching pants and reminded herself that she was a professional. She was used to dealing with people, even difficult people. She'd deal with this one.

She took one step toward the house when a man appeared in the doorway.

And Mary's heart stopped. Then started again with a very heavy thud.

The man, or Roman god, as Mary had instantly decided, frowned and walked back to the man in charge. His steps were brisk but very much controlled. His stride was quick but confident. As he frowned, Mary could see crinkles that formed at his eyes. Eyes that were a deep green, eyes that spoke of intensity, of purpose, of passion.

And the rest of the face wasn't too bad either. Light brown hair shone in the Florida sun, wavy and styled just so. Mary had an irrational urge to run her fingers through it. His lips were thinning as he was displeased and Mary wondered how they would look if he smiled. Or how they would feel if . . .

She shook her head and tried to concentrate. The head mover was pointing to her as she keyed in to his last words. " . . . said to stop."

The hot guy looked at Mary, giving her a once over. Then to her surprise, he dismissed her by saying, "You can finish the job," at which time the head mover motioned for his workers to continue working.

Mary's infatuation with the man came to a screeching halt. How dare he override her wishes at her own house. She looked around and seeing that the men were going back to work called out, "Oh, no. Everyone stop until we've got this settled." She imitated the head mover's motion and hollered, "Stop!"

Hot guy slowly turned to face Mary and in a haughty tone said, "Excuse me, but is there a problem?"

"Yes, there is," Mary said, straightening her shoulders and walking to stand in front of him. "This is my house and I don't like strangers ordering furniture and what not to be moved into it!"

Hot guy gave Mary another glance and then said, "Oh. You must be the head housekeeper. Good." He reached into his pocket and pulled out a piece of paper. "I'd like to go over the schedule that we'll be following for the next six weeks." He then proceeded to motion the movers back to work.

Mary stared at the paper now in her hand. When her voice came back it was low and concise. "I don't care about your schedule Mr. . . . whoever you are." She crumbed the paper and shoved it into her pocket. To look at later.

Mary yelled and motioned the movers to stop.

Hot guy's eyes glared at her for a moment and then he whistled and motioned, starting the movers back.

To which Mary yelled and motioned, stopping them. How she wished she could whistle.

This went back and forth several times as the workers looked beseechingly at their boss. Finally the man yelled, "Okay, men, let's take a ten minute break so these people can get everything sorted out." Then he looked at the two and muttered, "I have a schedule to keep so you two had better come to an understanding. In ten minutes we finish the job." He walked away to give them privacy.

When the boss was out of earshot, Mary balled her fists at her hips and speared "Adonis" with a glare. "Okay, pal, tell me who you are and why you're moving this stuff into my house."

"Perhaps I should speak with Mr. Swenson directly. Suppose you get him on the phone for me."

"Oh, don't worry. He's going to hear about this. But first I want to know where's the woman you came with?"

"She's organizing everything in the house."

When Mary headed toward the front door, he followed and said, "But I don't think she wants to be disturbed at the moment. Not while she's creating."

Mary rolled her eyes. "Oh please." She took a few more steps when he took her arm to stop her. Mary looked down at the offending arm and over-enunciating each word, said, "Unless you'd like to lose it, I suggest you move it."

He sniffed and said, "Threats, is it? Why am I not surprised?"

"Oh, pal. It'll be more than threats if you don't move your hand immediately."

They stared each other, eyes heating, tempers flaring when a bright, feminine voice sounded through the front door.

"Trevor? What's holding up the movers, darling?"

Mary jerked her arm away and turning saw a striking woman strolling their way. Even though she was in her early fifties, she had the figure of a twenty-year old. Her thick wavy blonde hair glided behind her as she stepped forward, her eyes laughing with delight.

She saw Mary and the eyes grew wider, the smile bigger. Her arms opened wide and she whispered, "Mary."

Mary swallowed hard. She couldn't stop the smile that came across her face as she walked to the woman. "Hi, Mom."

Trevor Crane was a man that liked to be in charge. He was very good at it. But at the moment he felt completely flummoxed.

He took another look at the girl, no, woman, that his employer was hugging. Why hadn't he seen it before? They looked so much alike. Same build, same blonde hair, same delicate features. And he'd called her the housekeeper. Well, it was an honest mistake. She wasn't dressed the part of

Merrilyn Kennedy Swenson's daughter. She wore a pants suit, for crying out loud. No jewelry to speak of, little makeup. And she'd handled the moving situation like a hoodlum, causing a scene. If she'd just told him at the start who she was, they could have escaped all the drama.

How was he to know this was Merrilyn's daughter, the one she constantly spoke about? However, from the way the woman always spoke of her, he would have guessed she was a young girl. Not an attractive woman of . . . oh, mid twenties.

He watched the two continue to hug and then break apart, both of them speaking at the same time, neither minding. He looked at his watch and decided to break up the happy reunion.

"Uh, Merrilyn. The men need to get back to work. That is, if everything's settled." He glanced at the daughter and back to Merrilyn.

Merrilyn gave her daughter one last adoring look and then put her arm around her. "Yes, you're right." Addressing her daughter, she said, "Sweetheart, I'd like for you to meet my . . . assistant. Trevor Crane. Darling, this is my little girl. Mary Swenson." Trevor gave Mary a polite but cool nod, which Mary ignored.

"What's all this about, Mom?"

Merrilyn replied, "I came to help you, of course. With the parade." She gave Mary another look and then enclosed her in another hug. "You need my help. Well, Mama's here." She kissed Mary's cheek and said, "Isn't this wonderful? I'll get to spend the holidays with you. Won't that be fun? We can go shopping together and attend the symphony and ballet. Just like when you were a little girl. And you and I will put together the best Christmas parade ever."

"Does Dad know about this?"

Trevor noticed Merrilyn's strained expression. "I, ah, haven't told him yet. I wanted it to be a surprise."

"Oh, he's going to be surprised, all right." Mary looked at the trucks. "Why all the furniture and stuff?"

"I wouldn't be comfortable without my things. Especially since I've decided to stay for a while. Now, let me get settled and then we can have a nice cup of tea and talk."

The expression on the daughter's face was comical. He almost felt sorry for the woman.

Merrilyn went outside, waving a delicate hand at the moving men. "Yoo hoo. Gentlemen. You can finish the work now. Everything's settled."

Trevor had the feeling that everything was far from settled. Family could complicate plans, as he well knew. He and Merrilyn were there to do a job, helping to put on a parade, and also, hopefully, to work on an important account, a wealthy philanthropist in Palm Beach. Trevor needed to be at his best. He needed the Christmas bonus Merrilyn had promised. Obstacles were not allowed, to his mind.

He followed Merrilyn back to the house as the daughter was pulling out her cell phone. He vaguely heard her say, "Dad? I think you should get home right away. We've got a . . . situation."

Probably the understatement of the year.

Chapter Three

Mary watched her father pace the long driveway in front of his huge home. The home that he'd lived in for many years, the last five without his wife.

Neither parent had ever told Mary what had happened between them. Mary only knew that one day her mother had moved to New York and started her own business of event planning for the philanthropic rich.

Since that day, Mary had tried to love both her parents, but they didn't make it easy. Her mother had insisted that she occasionally travel with her—Aruba, New Orleans, Lake Tahoe, while her father was adamant about Mary spending holidays with him. She felt torn, as if she never pleased either one.

Her father had seemed so lonely, she'd chosen to settle in Charity, with him. He needed someone to take care of him so she'd happily taken on that role. The hurt masked behind the frustration on his face even now made her want to go to him and give him a big hug. But she refrained, letting him work off his energy before the inevitable blowup.

As she watched her father trying to drum up the nerve to face his estranged wife, a wave of love washed over her.

She walked over and gently put her hand on his shoulder. "Why don't you just get this over with?"

Frank Swenson was a proud man. But for a second his eyes betrayed a vulnerability that had tears pooling in Mary's eyes. He looked briefly at his daughter and then at the house. His sigh was quiet and sad. "I guess you're right." He straightened and purposefully strode to the house.

With a confidence that Mary envied, Frank stood tall and purposefully walked towards the building.

Mary followed him, wanting to lend her support. They looked around the massive great room and then the kitchen but saw no one. Hearing a small laugh, they both headed to the pool in the backyard.

Frank opened the French doors that separated the breakfast nook from the back patio. He strode out, Mary closely behind and then stopped abruptly, causing her to bang into him.

She peered around him and saw her worst nightmare. Her mother, her *mother*, was stretched out on her side on a lounge chair, clad in a very sexy one-piece bathing suit. And her *assistant*, wearing swim trunks, was on his knees behind her lathering lotion on her back. Mary gulped. This did not look good. Did her mother bring her boy toy here to shove into her father's face?

Mary glanced at her dad to see how he was handling it.

His eyes seemed to drink in the woman, feasting on her beauty. As if she was too exquisite to be real. "Merry," Frank whispered.

He said it so quietly that Mary barely heard him. But her mother had. Her head turned to see her husband standing across the patio.

If Mary had been surprised by her father's expression, she was flabbergasted at her mother's. Merrilyn's eyes grew huge and a smile automatically tugged her lips, a genuine smile that made her appear as a shy, infatuated young woman. She edged away from Trevor, sitting straight, her hands on her lap. "Frank," she said breathlessly.

"Ah . . . you look . . . good."

Mary blinked twice at her father. He was actually stuttering. The man that was always in charge, that always knew what to say. What was going on here?

"Thank you," Merrilyn said softly, adding a slight giggle.

A giggle? Her mother? Had the earth suddenly slipped off its axis? Had the apocalypse arrived?

Mary frowned wondering if she should quietly slip out so these two *teenagers* could stare and giggle some more. Maybe she should insert herself so they came back to the here and now.

As she was mulling this over, her father said, "Well, it's been . . . I mean . . ." Suddenly Frank's eyes went hot and his chest filled up with air. "Merry Swenson. Would you kindly tell me what's going on?" Frank stomped toward the pool, his eyes firmly fixed on his wife.

"Sweetheart, it's so good to see you again." Merrilyn had also regained her balance. She sat up, curving her legs around her, as a good model would have. "Come give me a kiss."

His eyes hard, Frank turned his attention on Trevor. "Who are you?"

Trevor stood. "I'm Trevor Crane. Ms. Swenson's assistant." He extended his hand, which Frank looked at for an uncomfortable moment before shaking.

He turned back to Merrilyn and said, "I want to know why you're here bringing all your crap with you and disrupting our lives."

Mary knew the phrase "our lives" had a direct effect on Merrilyn. Frank was putting himself with her against her mother. Not good.

Merrilyn plastered a smile across her brightly painted lips. "Isn't it obvious? I'm an event planner, the best in New York. I came to help my baby with the big parade she's planning."

She sighed and added, "Besides Frank, is it bad for a mother to want to spend the holidays with her family?"

"You could have asked. Prepared us for your arrival."

Now Merrilyn's eyebrows rose. "And given you the chance to hightail it to the Bahamas for Christmas? Taking my daughter with you?"

"Bermuda," he replied, grinning at the idea.

"Just as I supposed. What's the matter, Frank? You afraid to spend Christmas with me? Plan to run away?"

"That's *your* specialty," he hissed.

Merrilyn's eyes hardened. She stood and folded her arms across her ample cleavage. "The reality is I am here for the season and I intend to enjoy myself immensely. *Your* attitude is up to you."

Her parents were both excellent poker players. She couldn't gauge what either of them were feeling, so she waited in the silence to see who laid down the next card.

Her father walked to face Merrilyn, his hands on his hips. "All right. But *he* doesn't stay here," Frank said, his eyes never leaving Merrilyn.

She looked over at Trevor and had the audacity to smile. "I thought he could stay in the apartment over the garage."

"That's my apartment," Mary said coming forward with a frown.

Trevor chuckled, and he gave her another of his disdainful looks. "You live in a garage apartment? Poor child."

Mary had never wanted to stick her tongue out at anyone more in her life. Of course she couldn't. She'd be acting on the "child" comment.

But in her mind that tongue was out.

"I want him down at the hotel. No discussion," Frank said narrowing his eyes.

Merry sighed, as if the matter was a minor irritation. "All right, if you're so determined about it."

Mary shook her head. The whole situation was getting on her nerves. The fringes of a headache were starting to make an appearance. She desperately wanted to be at work, the diner, anywhere but here.

"Fine." Frank stalked away as if he'd had the same idea as Mary.

"Oh, we will see both of you at dinner tonight." It wasn't a request. "Six o'clock. I'll handle everything. Please don't be late."

Frank didn't turn around. He merely slowed as if he were thinking about responding. Deciding against it, his steps quickened and he was gone.

Merrilyn's little chuckles brought Mary's attention back to her. She absolutely wanted to strangle her mother. How could she just show up, demanding that they be a family for the holidays? And with a boyfriend in tow? It was unconscionable.

"Mary, dear, how about getting your mother a diet drink?"

"Oh, I'll get that for you, Merrilyn." Trevor stopped as he approached Mary and under his breath said, "You live over a garage? I can't believe you're Merrilyn's little girl."

"No? Well, maybe this will help remind you."

Before Trevor could dodge, Mary pushed him with all her might, causing him to fall backwards into the pool. The splash was big, sending a spray of water over both Mary and her mother, who was now standing by her daughter.

Mary was mortified. How could she have done such a thing? That man had just made her so furious!

Trevor sputtered as he surfaced, his eyes blazing as he pushed his soaked hair back.

"You must admit, darling, you had that coming," Merrilyn said, obviously trying to hold back her mirth.

Mary knew she was blushing. Pushing a man, a stranger, into a pool was so unlike her. Usually she was pretty even keeled, a go-with-the-flow kind of girl. She stepped closer to the pool edge and said, "I am so sorry. That was . . . well, it was just inexcusable."

"Miss Swenson. You'd better be glad I was dressed for the pool. Otherwise, you'd be joining me," Trevor said as he swam to the edge, his strokes long and smooth.

Without words and totally embarrassed, Mary turned to leave but was stopped when her mother spoke.

"Mary, honey. After dinner I'd like you to drive Trevor to the hotel in town. I'll call them now so they'll have his room ready."

Great. Now she was going to have to spend more time with him. Alone. She wanted to refuse. She wanted to scream at her mother for bringing the man to begin with. Hadn't she seen how hurt her father was? But she wisely held her tongue and stomped away.

"Well, that was fun," Merrilyn said, doing a terrible job of disguising a grin.

"Yeah. Fun." Trevor wiped his face and hair. Maybe Merrilyn Louisa Kennedy Swenson was amused, but he was not.

Finally succumbing to her mirth, Merrilyn leaned back in her chair and chuckled. "Ah, this is just what I need to make the season interesting."

Trevor sat on the edge of her chair. "Don't tell me you're bored with the teas and dinners and parties scheduled in New York for the holidays."

"So incredibly bored, darling. All those Christmas events I'm expected to execute perfectly, all those holiday wishes to make come true." Her eyes took on a faraway look, with a wistful sheen.

"That's not like you, Merrily. You do your best work at Christmas."

"I . . . I think I needed a break this year. I'm so happy for the excuse to get away."

She seemed so sad. Merrilyn was always so lively, it was hard to see her this way. He decided to cheer her, so he shook his head, flinging pool water over her.

"Hey. I didn't want to get wet."

"Maybe you should have said something to that . . . *child* of yours." Trevor narrowed his eyes at Merrilyn.

She smiled. "All right, I may have led you to believe that my baby was a tad younger."

"A tad?" Trevor exclaimed. "She's a grown woman. I guess I should take back the teddy bear that I bought her as a Christmas gift."

Merrilyn grinned and glanced in the direction her daughter had taken. "Yes. She's a grown woman. And a very beautiful one at that."

"Yes. She is," Trevor said under his breath to which Merrilyn lifted an eyebrow.

Trevor gave a dignified shrug. "I notice these things." He leaned closer to Merrilyn and said, "Why, you two could be sisters."

Merrilyn chuckled and Trevor grinned, glad to have his vivacious employer back.

After all, they had work to do.

"Merrilyn," he said, thoughtfully. "As headstrong as your daughter seems to be, I'm sure she can handle a little parade. We should head south. I know that Benjamin Crandall is at his place in Palm Beach. It would be a good time to review the plans for his Valentine's Day fundraiser."

She breathed deeply and said, "No. I need to be here. To help Mary." She started to say something but then shook her head. "Mary needs my help."

"Are you sure? They don't seem too thrilled that we're here." When she turned her wide blue eyes on him, Trevor relented and said, "Okay, you want to stay. But how about I zip south while you're here with your family?"

"Oh no, Trevor. I need you here. I want this parade to be the very best. For Mary."

His brows furrowed. "But I don't know anything about the town. How am I going to help—"

"Darling. You are the best with research. I can help with that." She smiled slightly. "Charity is a wonderful little town. So much to offer." Her perfect brow lifted. "You know you're indispensable to me."

Just the position he wanted to be in, if he was to one day take over Merrilyn's business. "All right. Whatever you say. But might I suggest that we not work by the pool? Especially if your daughter is near."

Six o'clock came too early for Mary. At five till the hour she took two extra strength aspirin, pulled a light jacket around her ensemble of white cotton shirt and dark jeans, and headed for the main house.

Her father's Mercedes pulled up just as she was reaching the front door. Mary smiled knowing that he'd had the same idea—show up not a minute early. They talked for a few minutes outside before checking their watches and walking inside together.

The dining room of the Swenson home was hardly ever used. Mary's father thought it too formal and stuffy. He chose to eat his meals in the cheery breakfast room, where he could read his paper while looking through the back windows at the golfers that walked past, playing the town's golf course.

But when Mary and Frank walked into the house and viewed the formal dining room, they both had to grab each other to keep from bolting.

Merrilyn had been busy. A lacy tablecloth, ironed to perfection, had been placed over the mahogany table. There were china plates, cloth napkins in elaborate golden napkin holders, and more utensils than Mary knew existed. There were arrangements of poinsettias with tall white candles in crystal candlestick holders interspersed. Merrilyn was lighting them as they entered the room.

"Perfect," she said. "You two are right on time." She glanced at her daughter and crossed her arms. "Mary. Didn't I teach you to dress for dinner?"

"Sorry, Mom," she returned, not really sorry at all. "Must have slipped my mind."

Trevor came in with a bottle of wine. He gave a polite gaze toward Frank, looked down his nose at Mary, and poured four glasses of the vintage.

It was going to be a long night.

"Well, everything's ready. Shall we sit?" Merrilyn placed her hand on the back of her chair and lifted an eyebrow in Frank's direction. He rolled his eyes and pulled the chair out for her. "Thank you, darling."

She gave her napkin a snap and said, "Trevor, if you'd help Mary with her chair.

Mary watched him with suspicion. Once they all sat, Mary saw her mother reach for a little bell on the table and ring it briskly.

The swinging door to the kitchen pushed open and a short, solid woman with kind eyes wearing a starched black uniform hurried into the room. "*Da*, Mrs. Swenson?"

Mary was so surprised she couldn't speak.

"Elena, you may serve the first course now."

The older woman, that Mary guessed was in her sixties, went back to the kitchen, eager to please.

"Who's she?" Frank asked. "And where's Mrs. Appleby?" he asked referring to the Swenson's housekeeper.

"I brought Elena with me. She's a wonderful cook, trained at the Cordon Bleu in Paris. I put her up in the blue bedroom upstairs."

"Where's she from, Mom?" Mary asked.

"Moscow. Her accent is a little thick, but her *pirozhki* is divine. She also knows where to get the most excellent caviar."

"A must for any cook," Frank said sarcastically under his breath. Mary hid a chuckle. "What about Mrs. Appleby?"

"I gave her an extended vacation. Although I may ask her to serve for our big Christmas party."

Mary could see the pained look on her father's face. Their parties in the past had been legendary—elegant, delicious, fun. Warmth permeated Mary as she remembered as a young girl watching from the stairs when she was supposed to be in bed. The colors, the scents, the laughter. Remembering the annual Christmas party always put a smile on her face.

Apparently her father didn't feel the same way. He took a deep gulp of his wine, totally out of character for him.

"I like your Mrs. Appleby. She seems very . . . efficient," Merrilyn said gazing at Frank, who didn't notice.

Mary wondered at the hesitation in her mother's comment. And that look. Did she think her father was fooling around with . . . Mrs. Appleby?

It didn't make sense. Here her mother was showing off her own paramour. What did she care if her father was seeing anybody?

"She is," Mary said. "She pretty much does anything Dad asks her to do." Mary took delight in the brief confusion in her mother's eyes. *Serves you right.* As she snapped her own napkin and laid it in her lap, Mary added, "I don't know what we'd do without her. She's made the house a home." Merrilyn's face fell and Mary felt an instant of regret.

"How's the wine, Merrilyn?" Trevor said, clearly trying to ease the tension in the room.

After taking a sip, she said, "It's wonderful. Trevor, you really do know how to choose a good wine."

Elena brought out a platter with four small plates and placed each in front of the foursome. "Ah, what is this, Mom?"

"Why, it's escargot, dear. You've had it before. Don't you remember we used to go to that adorable little French bistro in Midtown?" To Mary's blank look, Merrilyn said, "Oh, you've forgotten. How disappointing."

All four begin to eat the delicate morsels before them and Mary had to admit that the appetizer was delicious. She glanced over at her father who was also enjoying the dish.

The comfortable silence was short-lived when Merrilyn said, "I took the liberty of planning our Thanksgiving feast for next week."

"Merry," Frank said. "Didn't you think we might have made plans?"

"Oh? And what would they be?"

"We were going to Hal's Place and eat with friends."

Merrilyn furrowed her brow. "Hal's Place. You mean the diner in downtown Charity? I'm surprised that it's opened on Thanksgiving. Anyway, you needn't go out. We'll have a huge feast right here."

"No," Mary tried to explain. "The diner's closed. We take a couple of dishes to share with our friends."

"Oh, a pot luck. How sweet," Merrilyn said returning to her food. Then she excitedly said, "I know. Why don't you invite everyone over here to join us?"

Frank sat back and eyed his wife. "No."

Merrilyn's eyes widened. "No?"

"You heard me. You can't suddenly show up and expect us to change all our plans at your whimsy. Now, if you'd like, we could ask Grace if it'd be okay for you to come."

"Grace? You mean Grace Hudson? Hal's daughter?"

"Yeah. She and her husband run the diner. Along with her mother and aunt. You remember

Ellen, Merry. Used to be Ellen Charles. She's Ellen Scott now. Married the mayor, Howard Scott."

Her voice softened as she said, "Really? I'd like to see her again. She was such a good friend." Merrilyn took a delicate bite of her appetizer, considering. "What about Trevor?"

Frank sighed and said, "He can come, too."

"And Elena."

"Her too," he said as Elena came back into the room to collect empty plates. "In fact, I'm sure everyone would love to eat some of her fancy Russian vittles."

Seeing that everyone was looking at her, Elena said, "*Shto*?"

Trevor immediately began speaking Russian to the woman who smiled and retreated back to the kitchen.

No one spoke as Elena returned with a soup course, a steaming French onion. Mary's mouth was salivating but before she could have a taste, Merrilyn said, "All right. Ask Grace if we can join them. And what we can bring."

It was a victory. A small one, but one nonetheless.

The main course of Chicken Dijon was served along with green bean almandine, sweet potato *pierogi* with sage brown butter sauce, and a sliced baguette.

The foursome ate in silence, a good thing, until Merrilyn said, "And when will I meet your young man, Mary?"

Mary swallowed hard. "My, ah, what?"

"Your young man. I know you're seeing someone. You've spoken of several dates with a . . . Brent? Brett?"

"Brad."

"Ah, Brad. So, when do I get to meet him?"

"I don't know, Mom. Brad is pretty busy right now."

"And what does he do for a living?" Merrilyn asked before taking another small bite.

"He's a scientist. He works in research and development for the Omega Consumables Corporation. And he teaches a few courses at the University of Central Florida."

"Impressive," Trevor said, surprisingly. "We've actually used some of Omega's products. They're very forward thinking in biodegradable, yet quality consumables."

"Sounds like quite a catch. Well done, my dear," Merrilyn said.

Mary did not like her tone. "We're . . . you know, not serious. Just seeing each other casually."

"Well, that's all right. I suppose. Just remember, aside from a shared intellect, which is a must, you want any potentially lasting relationship to have passion. The kind of passion that . . . that takes your breath away, that makes your heart pound. That puts a twinkle in your eye."

Mary's face began to heat. She quickly glanced to Trevor to see if he was listening, and of course he was. "I'd really rather discuss this later, Mom. When we're alone."

"Frank. What do you think about this Brad?" Merrilyn asked, turning her attention to the older man who was busy eating his delicious dinner.

"I think it's completely Mary's business, not ours." He took a sip of wine and then said, "We can trust her judgment." Frank winked at his daughter and went back to eating.

Mary tried to hide her sigh of relief. She knew that her dad was lukewarm at best about her dating Brad, but it meant the world to her that he was defending her choices.

"Fine. But I'd still like to meet the young man. Now, let's talk about your parade. I have a few ideas to get us organized."

Mary gave her mother a small smile and joined her father in eating dinner, letting Merrilyn go over her thoughts.

Feeling eyes on her, Mary looked across the table to see Trevor glaring at her. What was his problem?

Well, he'd just better cut a wide path around her this evening. She was in no mood to deal with the man. Unless they happen to be near the pool.

As she cut another piece of chicken, Mary let a grin cover her face.

Why did this girl bother him so much? Even now as she had a silly grin on her face, Trevor couldn't seem to take his eyes off her. Why?

She was nothing but a complication. His job was to assist Merrilyn, to become her indispensible right hand man so that he could easily slip into the presidency of Kennedy Swenson Events, the premiere planning company in Manhattan, a role he was ready for. Merrilyn was grooming him for it. She had intimated that it would only be a few years before she stepped down from her position, perhaps even sooner.

He still couldn't figure out her true motives for coming to this hick town for the holidays. She said it was to help her daughter with the town's parade, but he couldn't help the feeling that something else was going on.

Regardless, he'd do her bidding, follow her lead. He did wish, however, that he could talk her into setting up a meeting with Benjamin Crandall. The man had tons of money to plow into his big Valentine's Day gala and Trevor wanted to insure that the customer was satisfied. Crandall carried a lot of weight with other New York bigwigs. Trevor was excited at the prospects. And the hope of more money. Especially when his family needed it. The situation at his family's home was getting worse every day. He had to help.

Then his eyes connected with the fascinating blue ones of the woman sitting across from him. She had a graceful beauty, similar to Merrilyn, yet different. Her wavy golden hair was pulled back in a ponytail as it had been earlier, which seemed to cause her flawless face to stand out.

She really could have been a model, with her high cheekbones, big eyes, and warm smile. Not that she'd smiled at him, but the affection she obviously felt for her parents had her gifting them with the most attractive smile he'd ever seen.

Trevor looked back at his soup. No. No, no, no, no. He wasn't going to let a woman with a pretty face take his eyes off the goal. Especially when that woman was Merrilyn's daughter. How awkward would that be?

No, he'd continue doing his job to the best of his ability.

He didn't want to be in Charity, Florida for the holidays but he'd do it. For Merrilyn. He'd just have to ignore his basic instincts that said Mary Swenson was a woman worth getting to know.

Besides, she had a boyfriend. And in six weeks he'd be safely back in his apartment in Midtown Manhattan. Maybe he could head back a little early, in time to catch New Year's Eve in Times Square. He'd have to check his contact list for a date. Yeah, that's what he needed. A big date for New Years.

Trevor felt better as he took another bite of chicken. He always felt better when he had a plan.

Chapter Four

Mary drove Trevor back to the hotel after dinner, glad to get out of the house. In fact, she decided to stay away herself, let her parents have some time alone. She wondered if they'd kill each other. She wasn't going back anytime soon to find out.

Pulling up in front of the hotel, Trevor said, "Could you tell me where I could rent a car? Since your father won't let me stay at the house, I need a way of getting to Merrilyn." The phrasing caused Mary to clench her teeth.

"Well, if you need transportation only in town you can walk down the street to the NEV rentals."

"Neighborhood Electric Vehicle?" he said referring to the golf cart vehicles common throughout the streets of Charity.

Mary leaned away to study him. "You are just a barrel of knowledge, aren't you?"

"I'm flattered, really. But that is a good idea. That way I can get back and forth." The edges of his lips lifted just a bit. "I don't want to inconvenience you."

"Too late." Really, how could she have ever thought the guy handsome? His total demeanor completely irritated her. "The NEV office opens at ten in the morning." She returned the slight smile. "Too bad we'll miss you at breakfast."

"I'm devastated," he said as he shut the car door and disappeared into the hotel.

Mary drove around looking for a parking space. The man had her so riled, the last thing she wanted to do was go home.

She parked and headed to Hal's Place. A good, strong cup of coffee was what she needed. And maybe a friendly ear. Surely she could find a friend there.

The bell ringing atop the door as she entered instantly had her spirits lifting. Looking around she saw that the supper crowd had thinned and those wanting a late dessert and coffee had started to filter in.

"Well, hey there, sweetie."

Mary smiled and greeted Ellen Scott. "I'm surprised to see you, Ellen. You're not here too much anymore."

"I know. I don't get to work here as much as I used to, but Mac is out of town and Grace and Pauline wanted to go see a movie together so I told them I'd hold down the fort. You want a table, booth, or counter?"

"It's just me. The counter's fine."

Ellen served Mary a cup of coffee and said, "I heard there was big news out at your place today."

"Yeah," Mary said stirring her black coffee. "Mom's back."

"I take it this was very sudden?"

"Out of the blue." Mary sighed. "She brought half her apartment, her own cook, and . . . a handsome . . . *assistant.*"

Ellen poured herself a cup of coffee and sat next to Mary. "I see."

Mary hated the note of sympathy in Ellen's voice. "I'm sure it will be fine. It's just through December, although if Mom makes it through the holidays without the glitz and glamour of New York I'll be surprised."

Ellen took a sip. "You know, Mary. This may be a good thing."

"How do you figure?"

"Don't you think your parents need to talk? I mean, it's been . . . what . . . five years? I'd say they had things to settle between the two of them."

She thought about the situation and took a sip. "Yes. They do." Growing angry, she set her mug heavily on the counter. "But did she have to bring that . . . that man with her? I can't imagine how Dad's feeling."

"No, I don't suppose any of us can. But I know your father. He's a good man. I'm sure he's going to handle things."

They both sipped their coffee. "I will admit that I'm eager to see your mom." Ellen smiled warmly. "We were good friends before she left."

"Oh, that reminds me. Can she, the cook, and the guy come with us on Thanksgiving?"

"Why of course, honey. You don't even have to ask."

"I didn't want to put my friends in the midst of the drama that is my family."

Ellen chuckled and gave Mary a one-armed hug. "We've had plenty of our own. But if I've learned anything about family drama it's this . . ."

When she didn't continue, Mary turned to her. Ellen looked her square in the eye. "Don't jump to conclusions. About anything. Or anyone, for that matter."

As Mary thought about that, the door to the diner opened followed by laughter. Mary saw her friend Grace and her mother coming into the diner, arm in arm, giggling like schoolgirls. For a moment Mary was so envious. She wanted that with her mother. Yes, she loved her mother very much, but over the years Merrilyn Kennedy Swenson had become so . . . unapproachable. She couldn't imagine going to a movie with her and then hanging out in a diner laughing.

"Ellen, you won't believe the film that we just saw."

"I take it, it was entertaining?"

This led the women into another fit of laughter. Grace held her stomach and said, "I'll say. Especially when the hero took off his shirt and mom, my mother, said, 'Hubba hubba,' out loud. I thought I'd die laughing."

"What can I say? I am a connoisseur of fine specimens."

Ellen smiled. "So you had a good time. I'm glad. Mary was just keeping me company."

Seeing her friend, Grace said, "Hey, Mary. What's going on? You okay after what happened today?"

Small towns, she thought. Everyone already knew what was going on. "I'm okay."

"Well, since you're back, Pauline, I'll let you take over. I'm going home to Howard," Ellen said and then waved her farewell.

"I'll get to work then," Grace's mother said. "Since that hero got me worked up." Grace and Mary giggled. "Good to see you, Mary."

"You, too." Mary observed Grace watching her mother, her eyes shining. "It's good to see you and your mom together."

"Yeah. It's a real miracle." Grace poured herself a cup of coffee and leaning over the counter said, "Which makes me want to know about your day."

Mary sighed heavily. The last thing she wanted to do was rehash the whole rotten day. But she treasured Grace's friendship and her insight so she did just that.

Grace cut them each a slice of chocolate cake and listened while Mary poured her heart out.

"Wow," Grace said, eating another bite of cake. "That's a lot to deal with."

"You should know." Mary ran her fork through the luscious cake, for which she had no appetite. "I guess I should be thankful she's going to help me with the parade, but . . ."

"Yeah. But."

"You've been through difficulties with your mom. How do you get through something like this?"

Grace pursed her lips and looked thoughtful. "I think you try to be wise. Listen." Her eyes softened as she said, "And vent to a good friend over chocolate cake."

Mary laughed. "I love you, Grace." She filled her fork and took a huge bite of chocolate. "Almost as much as I love this cake." She grinned.

They continued to chat, about the parade, about Thanksgiving, about the movie Grace had seen, until closing time grew near. Mary watched a few remaining customers leave and Grace take care of their cups and plates.

Her eyes were drawn to the huge windows, to the people walking outside. To her surprise she saw a familiar face. It was him.

Now what was he up to so late at night?

"You want me to walk you out? Hey, what are you looking at?"

"It's him! Right there! It's the jerk my mother brought!"

Grace stood next to her. "Wow. Too bad my mother didn't see him." When Mary stared at her, Grace said, "I mean, come on. You've got to admit that is one nice looking man."

Mary shrugged and tried to look indifferent. "If you go for that kind, I guess."

Grace snorted.

"Come on!" Mary grabbed her purse and pulled Grace with her.

"Where are we going?"

"To follow him."

"What?"

In front of the diner Mary stopped. "If this man is involved with my mother, I want to know where he'd be going at eleven at night."

Grace gently touched her arm. "I understand that, Mary. But your mother's a big girl. It's her life. Are you sure you want to get involved in this?"

"If it was your mother, Grace, would you want to know?"

Grace took less than a moment to decide. She linked her arm with Mary's and said, "Well, let's do it."

They didn't have to go far. Trevor walked into The Tavern, a bar and grill in town that stayed open until two in the morning.

The girls entered, trying to keep hidden until they'd seen where Trevor went. Grace pointed when she saw him take a seat at the large mahogany bar in the center of the room.

Mary pulled her to a small booth in the corner where she could keep an eye on him.

"Now what are we going to do?" Grace asked as she waved to several people she knew.

"Just keep an eye on him."

"He's sure to see us. Oh look, there are the Holbrooks. I didn't know they were in town." Grace waved to a couple on the other side of the bar.

"Could you stop? You're drawing attention to us. Here," Mary said handing Grace a menu. "Hold it up in front of your face."

Obeying her, Grace muttered, "Then how are we supposed to watch him?"

Mary lowered the menu slightly to view Trevor. He was talking to the bartender, Sven, if Mary remembered correctly.

"Hey Mary. Grace. What can I get for you?"

The women looked up to see a tall redhead standing by their booth, pad and pencil at the ready.

"Hey, Sally. How's it going?" Grace said.

"Not too bad. Paul's doing a gig in downtown Orlando tonight, so I'm doing a double shift."

Grace smiled at the former waitress from Hal's Place, who had eloped with a talented saxophone player. "I bet the tips are pretty good here."

Before Sally could answer, Mary broke into the little reunion. "See that guy in front of Sven? What's he drinking?"

Sally glanced at the bar, then turned back to the women. "Looks like an Irish coffee. You want one?" she asked ready to write the order.

"No, I . . . ah, okay, maybe one. Grace?"

"Nothing for me. I'm just keeping you company."

Sally left and then Grace said, "Now what?"

"Menus back," Mary said as Trevor turned slightly. She peeked over just in time to see a long-legged brunette take the seat next to him. "Okay, now let's see what you do, Mr. Know-It-All. Gonna impress the lady with your knowledge?"

"You know these onion rings look really good," Grace said. "Maybe we should add them to our menu."

Trevor and the brunette started laughing. "He's flirting! He's definitely flirting! Would you look at the nerve at that guy? My poor mother."

"Really, do you think onion rings would sell at Hal's Place?"

"Grace, pay attention. My mother's boyfriend is making a move on some girl at the bar. What should I do?"

"I think you should relax. The girl's flirting with Sven now."

Mary took a chance to turn toward the bar and when Trevor moved, cried, "Menus up!"

No one spoke, as Mary tried to will her heartbeat to slow. Surely Trevor hadn't seen her. "What do you think? Do we look again?"

Grace didn't respond and Mary peered around her menu. "Grace? Grace?" She rapped on the menu finally getting the woman's attention.

"Sorry. Just checking out their menu. I love the artichoke dip and gourmet cracker combination. I guess it's a little high brow for Hal's, huh?"

"Grace. Help me out, will ya?"

"You keep telling me to look at the menu!" Grace dropped the menu onto the table. "Why should I hide anyway? He doesn't know me from Adam."

"Good point. Okay, you look and let me know what's going on. Any more women around him?"

"No. Ah, he's talking to Sally. No, I think he's talking to Sven. I really can't tell from here. You want me to sit at the bar and eavesdrop?"

"Maybe. Let me think . . ."

Sally walked up, a smile on her face placing the coffee, heavy on cream, in front of Mary. "Here's your drink."

"Thanks. What do I owe you," Mary said pulling out her purse.

"Oh, no charge. It's compliments of the hottie at the bar." Sally gave Mary a wink, grinned at Grace, and walked away.

Mary's head jerked around to see Trevor, his back against the bar, a smug grin on his face as he stared at her. He lifted his glass in salute.

She was totally and completely embarrassed.

Turning away from him, she slumped down into the cushioned booth as her face heated, probably turning beet red.

"I guess the jig's up, huh?" Grace said trying to hold back a chuckle. "It's not so bad, honey. You can always say that we came in for a drink and had no idea he was here. It's nothing so—oh, my gosh! He *is* a hottie!"

Mary smirked at her friend.

"I mean, you said he was good looking, but you didn't say like movie star, sexy model good looking."

"Yeah, he's okay. Why are you just now noticing that?"

"Because I'm getting a better look at him since he's coming over."

Chapter Five

While Mary grimaced, Grace smiled widely. "Hello, you must be Trevor Crane. I'm Grace McCrae." She held out her hand to shake.

Trevor graced her with a sincere smile as he took her hand. "Pleasure to meet you, Grace." He glanced at Mary and added, "I hope you won't believe everything you've heard about me."

"I never trust first impressions. Neither do you, right Mary?"

Mary looked up at her friend as Grace lifted her eyebrows at her. "Of course not, Grace." Her attention went to the man standing next to them and her heart did a jump. She reprimanded herself—she didn't like this man, not at all. He was involved. With her mother.

It was anger, that's what it was.

"Well, I know you want to thank Trevor for the drink so I'll just be going now," Grace said as she slid out of the booth. "Trevor, nice to have you in Charity. Please come by Hal's Place and try our food while you're here."

"Grace, where are you going?"

"I'm going home and wait for Mac's call. Mac, that's my husband," she said in explanation to

Trevor. "He's out of town on business. Well, see you two." She left, smiling.

Trevor sat in Grace's place and sipped his drink, as did Mary.

Neither spoke for a moment. The silence was killing Mary. "You didn't have to buy my drink, you know," she murmured.

Trevor lifted one brow. "I think the words you're looking for are 'Thank you for the drink, Trevor.'"

Grinning into her drink, she said, "Thank you for the drink, Trevor. But you didn't have to. No use trying to get on the daughter's good side."

"Maybe I just wanted to help you quench your thirst after following me." He grinned widely.

"Following you? Hey, Grace and I just came in to get a drink. I was not following you."

Trevor turned to the bar. "It's a lovely establishment, this tavern. I especially like the mirror that surrounds the back of the bar. In fact, it shows everything that's happening behind those sitting at the bar."

Mary slowly looked over and cringed. Could the evening get any worse?

"I know that we started out on the wrong foot—"

"You mean since you invaded my house and thought I was the housekeeper?"

Trevor had the nerve to chuckle. "Yes. Being the daughter of Merrilyn Kennedy Swenson, I'm sure that would irritate you."

"And that means?"

"Just that Merrilyn doesn't like to be taken by surprise, nor does she ever want to be mistaken for the housekeeper."

Mary took a sip and then said, "Know my mother pretty well, do you?"

"Not as well as I'd like. For instance, her name. Your father kept calling her 'Merry.' But that also happens to be your name. Any explanations?"

"Yes, you heard my father . . . *her husband*, call her Merry. That's what he's always called her. He said she reminded him of a bright and beautiful Christmas. A 'Merry' Christmas." Mary looked down to hide the pain that ached in her chest. They had been so happy once. A happy family. Her eyes moistened as she remembered.

"And you're also Merry?"

"Mary with an 'a' one 'r' instead of 'e' double 'r.' Dad wanted to name me after Mom and she insisted that my name be spelled differently so it wouldn't be so confusing."

Mary drew a breath to control her emotions, took a sip of her drink, and sat up, her eyes looking around the bar. She did not want to gaze at the man that was possibly keeping her parents apart.

"Well, Mary with an 'a' one 'r.' It's been a long day. I think I'll call it a night." Trevor finished his drink, stood, and said, "How about I walk you to your car?"

"That's not necessary."

"No, I insist. It's late. I'd feel better if I knew you made it to your car safely."

She wanted to tell him that Charity wasn't New York City but refrained. It was kind of chivalrous of him. Another part of her wanted to see if he was the type of man who'd hit on her, while romancing another. "Okay." She took one more sip and slid out of the booth.

They walked in the silence of a November night in the little town. Mary could feel herself relaxing a little after what had been an emotionally draining day.

"So, you like Charity?" Trevor asked, sticking his hands in his pocket.

"What? Oh, yes. I like it very much."

"Better than New York? Amazing. I understand that you attended Columbia University. Merrilyn told me this afternoon. Can't imagine why you'd live here after experiencing the Big Apple."

Her back straightened as she felt the need to defend her hometown. "Charity doesn't have the energy of New York, that's for sure. But it's got . . . peace, heart, love."

"And nosy neighbors." Trevor chuckled. "I must have been asked a dozen times how 'Merry Swenson' is and how long we'll be in Charity. Word gets around fast."

"That it does." Mary looked down the main street that she loved. Her heart softened as she looked at the different stores, quiet, as if sleeping, resting up to serve the community the next day. "And the holidays are beautiful here. After Thanksgiving, the town will come together and turn this street into a beautiful Christmas painting.

It will be lit up like nothing you've ever seen. There will be hayrides, carriage rides, Santa Claus, ice skating, snow. It will—"

"Hold on a minute." Trevor stopped in the middle of the street. "You're telling me that it will snow? Here? In Central Florida?"

Mary loved extolling the virtues of Charity. It made her an excellent real estate agent. She smiled and said, "Absolutely. But it's actually Florida snow."

"Florida snow?"

"Yes. You'll just have to see it to believe it."

Trevor stuck his hands back in his pockets and said, "It can't be as pretty as New York at Christmas."

They began walking again. "Well, seeing as I've lived in both, I can say that you're wrong. Although I do miss a lot about New York."

"Why'd you really leave New York?" he asked quietly.

Mary looked straight ahead, feeling a stab in her heart. "Because my dad needed me."

They walked on in silence and Mary was grateful that Trevor didn't continue the conversation.

A light breeze ruffled her hair and as she turned to push it back, she got a view of Trevor's profile.

She could understand her mother's interest in this man, or any breathing female's, for that matter. His rugged face was softened by a patrician nose and deep green eyes that always seemed to be deep in thought.

His body wasn't muscular, but it wasn't soft either. It was lean with the benefit of youth. He had to be about her age, maybe a few years older, but definitely mid to late twenties. Possibly thirty.

My mother should be ashamed of herself.

Trevor suddenly glanced in her direction and Mary felt a blush creeping on her face at being caught staring. Thankfully the streetlights weren't too bright so maybe he wouldn't notice.

"My car's just this way," she said, leading him through an alley by the shops to a secluded parking lot.

She pushed the unlock button on her key ring and heard the familiar "beep, beep" of her car. The moment seemed awkward to her, as if coming to the end of a first date when you didn't know what to do or say.

Mary quickly shook that thought away. "Thanks. I can take it from here."

She was shocked when Trevor lightly took her arm and looked deeply into her eyes. The green of his eyes made her think of a churning sea as a storm approached. She was mesmerized.

"Listen. I know there's a lot of tension in your family. I get that. But could you please try to make this a good holiday for Merrilyn? She wants that more than anything."

Mary blinked and looked away. How could she forget for a second what was going on here? Her mother's boyfriend was asking her to get along. As if she were some bratty, spoiled child that just wanted her way.

She swallowed and stepped away from him. "I don't know if you believe this, Mr. Crane, but I love my mother. Yes, I was surprised when she just showed up, but that doesn't negate my love. However, I also love my father and am not looking forward to how this affects him."

"Your parents have much to discuss. In fact, in my opinion it's way overdue."

Mary's irritation rose, if that were possible. "You think so? I don't know who you think you are, but I'm not too happy about *your* being here. Why are you here anyway?"

"Merrilyn needed me. We have work to do."

"I'll just bet." Tears scalded the back of Mary's eyes as she quickly got into her sedan. Before she slammed the door she couldn't resist one more parting comment, something she'd been wanting to say to him as soon as she realized who he was.

"And don't even think about having me call you 'Dad.'"

Before she lost it, she cranked the engine and hurried out of the parking lot, not noticing the tears that streamed down her cheeks.

So, the man was concerned about the holidays. Okay, she'd make it the best in the history of holidays. She'd be accommodating, pleasant, gracious.

And she'd try with all her might not to punch Mr. Trevor Crane in his pretty face.

Trevor stood in the parking lot, his hands on his hips, his brow furrowed. *What is wrong with that girl?*

He shook his head as he walked to his hotel. She was the most confusing, irritating woman he'd ever met. All he was trying to do was to help his employer and good friend, and she goes ballistic on him. If she'd stayed a second longer it looked like she'd start crying.

Trevor let his mind meditate on what just happened. They'd been having a fairly pleasant conversation, something he wasn't sure was possible after their initial meeting. He'd been nice to her, bought her a drink, walked her back to her car. Even expressed his concern about her mother. Shouldn't that endear him to her instead of causing her to storm off in a mood?

His eyes softened as he thought about the moment when he took her arm. She'd looked up at him with the biggest eyes he'd ever seen. They'd captured his attention and he'd had to look slightly away to complete his thought.

Why did Merrilyn's daughter have to be . . . stunning. So naturally beautiful that he had to work at regulating his breath when he saw her.

He'd gone in to the bar to relax, to try to get her out of his head. And then she followed him in. Trevor laughed at loud. It was very satisfying to see her flustered at being caught.

And what was that crack about calling him 'Dad'? To do that he's have to . . . A wide smile crossed his lips as his steps hastened. *Oh, this is too good.* He laughed as he neared his hotel. *She thinks I'm . . . and that . . . and when Merrilyn said, and I said . . .*

Trevor bent over to hold his sides as the laughter continued. Every interaction of the day with Mary now made sense.

He walked through the lobby and entered the elevator, frowning at a new thought. Did Merrilyn know that her daughter, and now that he thought about it probably her husband, was thinking that he was her boyfriend?

His eyes narrowed as realization sunk in. Of course Merrilyn knew. She knew everything that happened in her orbit. As always, she was manipulating circumstances to fit her purposes, which usually didn't bother him.

But her manipulation had never involved him personally before.

The elevator doors opened and he walked slowly to his room. What was her objective? Why hadn't she discussed it with him? Most importantly, what should he do about it?

Trevor opened his door and walking in sat heavily on his bed. He unbuttoned the top two buttons of his shirt and rubbed his neck, thinking.

Merrilyn had been very good to him. She'd seen his potential, and, despite his lacking resume, had taken a chance on him as her assistant. He'd always be grateful.

But the last thing he wanted was to get mixed up in any family squabbles. Especially one that concerned a certain "Mary with an 'a' one 'r.'"

He shook his head as he stood and headed for the bathroom. His stay in Charity would be short and soon he'd be heading back to N.Y.C. And nothing was going to stop his plans for the future. Someday he would be running Kennedy Swenson Events. So he'd just play along with Merrilyn's game in the meantime, let the daughter think anything she likes.

Trevor sighed as he brushed his teeth. Although it would be hard to ignore those large blue eyes and that wavy blonde hair.

Chapter Six

Hal's Place was the spot in downtown Charity to go for casual meals, a pleasant atmosphere, nice people, and of course, the latest gossip. But on Thanksgiving it was a place for family and friends. And tons of scrumptious food.

As soon as Mary walked through the doors of the little diner, she was hit with the tantalizing aromas of turkey, stuffing, green bean casserole, and an array of pies—pumpkin, peanut butter, and pecan. Her mouth watered as she brought in her own humble offering of whipped mashed potatoes.

Smiles and hugs were mixed in with greetings as she and her dad moved around the dining room. She turned to see Merrilyn followed by Elena, each carrying a dish.

Mary put hers down and went to help the other women. To tell the truth, she was a bit nervous about how the others would react to her flighty mother being back in town.

She should have known better.

"Well, Merry Swenson, if you aren't a sight for sore eyes." Ellen Scott immediately came over, taking Merrilyn's dish, setting it down, and giving her a big hug.

"Ellen Charles. It's so nice to see you," Merrilyn said, as she returned the hug with the same enthusiasm. "Oh, I heard it's not Charles anymore."

"No, it's Ellen Scott now." She took Merrilyn's hand and said, "Let me introduce you to my husband, Howard."

Merrilyn looked back at Elena and before she could say anything, Mary said, "Go on, Mom. Elena and I will take care of the food."

Merrilyn gave her an appreciative smile and walked away with Ellen, as the woman chatted, catching up with each other.

Mary smiled. Why in the world had she worried about this? Of course Charity would open its arms and embrace her mother. That's the kind of town it was. And she loved it very much.

The door behind her opened and Trevor walked in carrying a bottle of wine. Looking more gorgeous than ever. Her heart did a flip-flop in her chest.

Why did the man do that to her? His casual look of pressed navy pants and collared Lacoste polo shirt wasn't sexy in the least. But on him? Mary had to swallow so that she wouldn't drool. His hair, the color of a delicious iced coffee, was slightly mussed, the result of the wind that had picked up.

Then to top if all off, Trevor smiled. Mary could feel her knees weakening. *Stop it!* she reprimanded herself.

"Miss? Where do I take this?"

Elena's question brought her back to the present. "Oh, I'm sorry. We'll go set these down and I'll introduce you to everyone." Mary led the way into kitchen where she and Elena left their food with a cheerful Pauline Hudson, who was manning the kitchen. Mary introduced Elena and while the two chatted, she returned to the dining room.

As she was about to push the swinging door that separated the two rooms, it swung toward her and Trevor entered. Suddenly they were facing each other, measuring each other.

They hadn't spoken in the past few days, not since he'd walked her to her car. Now as Elena and Pauline were involved in checking on the massive turkeys, they were virtually alone. And neither knew what to say.

A slow grin spread across his face as he gave her a once over before meeting her eyes. "I was told to leave this in here," he said, apparently enjoying Mary's discomfort. The rat.

"Yes." Mary turned and said over her shoulder, "Just follow me."

She introduced Trevor to Pauline as her mother's *assistant* and tried not to choke on the word. Then before things got awkward, she led Trevor back to the dining room so she could pawn him off on her mom.

Mary loved Thanksgiving at Hal's Place. What a wonderful group of people. It was such a nice mix—Ellen and her husband Howard, Grace and Mac, Mary's cousin Ross and his family, wife

Joy, seventeen-year old son Noel, and nine-year old Holly.

Urns of sweet iced tea and hot coffee were made available as everyone munched on light appetizers of spinach-artichoke dip (Grace had gotten the recipe from The Tavern) with crackers and raw vegetables.

The door opened and a loud cheer erupted as Big Jed and Little Jed made their way into the diner, each carrying a large covered pan.

"The crescent rolls are here! Now our feast is complete!" Grace called out, clapping her hands.

The Jeds put their pans down and removed their sweaters and hats, both grinning like loons. "Well, it is our specialty," Big Jed said.

"Yeah, just open the container and put the dough in the oven," Little Jed said laughing.

"It was still wonderful of you two to bring them," Ellen said. "I'll take them back to Pauline in the kitchen."

"I'll take them, Ellen. Keep your seat," Little Jed said as she started to stand.

"Let me help you, son," Big Jed said, grabbing one of the pans, while the others went back to their conversation and appetizers.

As they walked to the kitchen, the door opened and Pauline and Elena came into the room, having heard the arrival of the men.

Big Jed looked up and froze.

Elena froze.

While the two stood looking at each other Pauline glanced at Little Jed who returned the glance and shrugged.

"Ah, Big Jed. Have you met Elena?" Mary asked. Big Jed gave a barely perceivable shake of the head. "Oh, well may I present Elena Petrova. Mom brought her from New York. Elena, these are two of our favorite Charity citizens. Big Jed and his son Little Jed."

Big Jed slowly stepped forward and reached out, forgetting that his hands still held a pan of bread. Just as slowly, Elena took the pan. Their eyes continued to hold each other.

"Daddy?" Little Jed said.

"Nice to meet you . . . Elena," Big Jed murmured.

The woman nodded.

Mary tried to hide a smile.

Pauline put her hand on Elena's back said, "Why don't we get this bread in the kitchen and keep it warm." She took Little Jed's pan and carefully maneuvered Elena into the kitchen.

An hour later, the group sat at the large table set up in the dining room. Cheers went up when the two turkeys were placed in the middle of the table, emitting the aroma of succulent sausage stuffing.

"Two turkeys?" Trevor murmured to Merrilyn.

"That's right," Ellen said. "One for us and one for the Jeds."

Everyone laughed as they took their seats. Mary was fascinated that Big Jed moved quickly to pull out a chair for Elena. She was equally shocked when Trevor appeared behind her to pull out her chair. "Thank you," she said.

"You're welcome." His smile had her stomach flipping which she was not happy about. She immediately looked around the table to regain her composure.

Mac got everyone's attention and said, "Let's take hands and give thanks." He led the table in a prayer of thanksgiving for being together for another year, everyone's health, and the bounty before them.

Then the food was passed around with exuberance and humor.

Mary enjoyed the hum of conversations all around her. Holly was asking Grace about the supply of Christmas candy that Hal's Place would be carrying that year. Big Jed was listening rapturously to Elena struggle with her English, telling him about her home country. Trevor was seated next to Joy and was speaking fluent French, to which Joy happily replied.

The man knew French also?

Since she knew the language, she strained to hear bits of the conversation but unfortunately, they were a little too far away.

Her ears tuned into a comment from her mother that had her head turning. "Yes, I'm helping Mary with the big parade."

Mayor Scott said, "That's wonderful. I know it's going to be an entertaining event for our guests. Tell me, how's it going?" Everyone turned to Mary.

Ugh! She didn't want to explain that planning was in the beginning stages. And that her mother would be helping her. And Trevor. She really wanted a day off from tension. If only.

She thought quickly and cleared her throat. "I'd like to have a table at the town's decorating party and start getting sign-ups. I figured we'd keep the same route as the Fourth of July parade, keep it simple."

"You can put Hal's Place down for something, Mary," Grace said.

She smiled, grateful for her friend's support.

"Yeah. And as I'm sure you're going to have a Santa, I'll volunteer," Big Jed said and then seeing little Holly's big eyes added, "Since the real one's going to be busy getting ready for his big trip."

"That's great. Thanks."

"And this being Florida I think we should have something special pulling the sleigh. I mean, since we ain't got no reindeers down here."

"Like what?" Mary asked before she could stop herself.

The whole table was silent as everyone thought about the question. Finally, Holly piped out, "How about dolphins? That's real 'Floridy.'"

"That's not bad," Mary said wondering where they could get large plastic animals to attach to a sleigh.

"And we could bring in big aquariums to hold them," Holly said.

"Wait, what?"

Holly's brother Noel chuckled. "Cool. I'd pay to see that."

"I don't think you could do that," Little Jed commented. "You might get all them animal rights folks upset."

"But all they'd be doing was swimming, son. They wouldn't really be pulling the sleigh." Big Jed chuckled.

"That would be beautiful," Merrilyn said. "Perhaps we could add a sound system to hear their delightful calls."

Everyone added his or her own ideas, each one more ludicrous. Mary put her elbow on the table, and pinched between her eyes. So much for a tension-free day.

After the feast, which included a healthy helping of desserts, Ross Jackson announced that they were having a friendly football game at a local park and everyone was invited to participate.

"Give me a few minutes to run home and change and I'm in," Mary called out.

She saw the smirk from Trevor before he walked over to her. "You? Football?"

Not taking the bait, she said, "Are you joining? Or are you afraid you'll get your polo shirt dirty?"

"Oh, I'll be there. You'd just better hope that they put us on the same team, Miss Swenson. Unless you enjoy getting tackled." The edges of his lips lifted slightly and she thought she saw a split second of fire in his eyes. A shiver went down Mary's spine. Was he flirting with her? Or was it a threat? Maybe both.

She cleared her throat and said, "Let me get my mother home so she can rest and then I'll show you how to play football."

"No need for that, honey," Merrilyn said, appearing as if out of nowhere and wrapping her arm around Trevor's. "I'll just stay here and talk with the girls." She chuckled. "It's so good to see Ellen after all these years and I'm enjoying getting to know Pauline and Joy."

Merrilyn glanced behind her and added, "And I don't think Elena is ready to leave yet."

Trevor and Mary's gaze followed to see Elena and Big Jed sitting together chatting and laughing.

"Don't worry about me, Trevor. I'll be fine here and when I'm ready to go home, I'll walk." Seeing his concern she said, "It's only a little over a mile. Piece of cake."

"Argh, don't mention any food just now," Frank said joining the little group.

"You joining us for football, Dad?" Mary asked putting her arms around his middle.

"You betcha, pumpkin. Can't let you have all the fun." He gave her a kiss on the forehead.

Frank's expression turned to a scowl as he faced Trevor. "You going to join us, young man?" Mary couldn't help the smile that formed on her face hearing her dad put Trevor in his place.

"Yes, I think I will. There's not any age limit I take it?" he said, putting in his own dig.

"That's all right. I think they'll still let you play." He gave his daughter a wink and walked away.

Mary could not have been prouder of her dad.

Trevor walked around downtown Charity, still a little sore from the intense football game of the day before. The competition had been heated. His ribs ached from the dig Frank had "accidentally" given him. His foot had a bruise where Mary with an "a" one "r" had stomped. "Accidentally," of course. All in all, it had been a lot of fun.

The downtown area of Charity was unlike anything he'd ever seen, now as the whole town had turned out to decorate. Growing up in Brooklyn as one of seven children, holidays, although a big deal, always included putting in a lot of hours in his dad's small grocery store. Christmas was work, in his mind. He never had much time for just enjoying the season.

But in this little town, that's what everyone seemed to do. He strolled, hands in his pockets, watching storeowners hang lights outside. Citizens decorated the small downtown park along with the palm trees that lined the streets. The decorations just kept coming.

But Hal's Place outdid them all. It was covered in lights, garland, greenery, red bows, candy canes, Nativity, Santa and reindeer . . . you name it, it was there. Trevor especially liked the three stars that hung over the diner, brightly lit. During dinner yesterday someone had mentioned there was a story behind the stars and all the decorations at the diner. He'd have to get someone to tell it to him.

Around the giant Christmas tree that stood at the entrance to Main Street others were gathered, hanging ornaments and tinsel. A cherry picker was parked next to the tree holding a lone man, who decorated the upper regions. Trevor stopped to watch him as he placed an ornament while pushing his glasses back up on his nose.

The man pulled out a handkerchief and sneezed. *Allergies, really? From an artificial tree?* The man's attention went to the crowd and a smile lit his face as he waved to someone in the crowd. *Probably his mother.*

Curiosity getting the best of him, Trevor turned to see the object of his attention and nearly choked on his breath to see Mary Swenson waving back. Could this be the boyfriend?

Trevor walked over to stand next to Mary as she watched the tree being decorated. "You here to cheer on Prince Charming?" he asked nodding to the man in the picker.

"That's Brad. I wouldn't call him Prince Charming since that's a fictional character. You've been reading too many fairy tales."

Trevor grinned. He did like sparring with this woman. "You still sore after yesterday's football game?"

"What makes you sure I'm sore at all?" she asked keeping her eyes on the Christmas tree.

"Maybe it was the way you limped off the field."

Mary's eyes sparkled. "At least I wasn't bleeding. Finally got that to stop, did you?"

Trevor frowned. It was just a scratch. He cleared his throat and said, "Why wasn't Prince Charming at the game yesterday?"

"He was spending the day with his mother."

Figures, Trevor thought with a perverse satisfaction.

"Too bad. Well, maybe next time." Silence flowed between the two, as well as the tension. "But I must give him credit. Takes a brave man to get up in one of those cherry pickers."

"This is the first year we've used it. Before we've had men on stilts that put the ornaments up. But we had to stop it after one broke his leg when an ornament rolled under his stilt shoes and he fell." Trevor held back a chuckle. "Then last year nobody volunteered to do it so the upper half of the tree just had the lights that are permanently attached." He bit his lip to hide a laugh. "It seemed lacking so Mayor Scott brought in the cherry picker. What?"

Trevor shook his head and swallowed so he wouldn't laugh out loud. "Nothing. Interesting town, that's all."

He could feel Mary tense. "No, it's not New York. But it's a nice town. In fact, it's pretty wonderful. The perfect temperature. Laughter all around, beautiful lights, aromas of freshly baked cookies and ground coffee. It's pretty darn close to heaven, if you ask me."

Trevor didn't reply as Brad lowered himself and Mayor Scott walked to the microphone in front of the tree. "Howard's going to speak?" he asked nodding toward the man.

"He'll just say a few words and then the tree will light up and the snow will start."

"Can't wait," Trevor murmured. As the mayor spoke, Trevor watched to see if Brad would come and stand next to his girlfriend for this momentous holiday moment. Apparently Brad was needed by the tree in case of emergency, such as a loose fuse. Horrors.

Trevor chanced a glance over to see Mary concentrating on what the mayor was saying instead of looking at her boyfriend. He agreed with Merrilyn. It didn't look like any love match to him.

He shook his head. None of his business. He only wanted to get through the next few weeks, do a good job, and get back home.

His attention came back to the moment as the mayor started the countdown along with the many residents standing by. Bright lights all over the twenty-foot tree came on to the loud cheers and applause of the crowd. Seasonal music started from loud speakers along with a narration of a holiday tale set in the town of Charity. Children ran into the closed off main street to stand waiting with breathless anticipation. Confused, Trevor turned to Mary. She smiled and said, "Just wait for it."

As the story ended and the music built to a loud crescendo, boxes attached to the streetlights rumbled and emitted a white substance into the air. Children squealed, dogs barked, adults applauded as the atmosphere thickened with the matter.

Mary grabbed Trevor's hand and led him out into the middle of the street. She stretched out her arms as the white matter landed on her hair, her face, her clothes.

Trevor stared at Mary waiting for her to return his look. "Really? Soap bubbles?"

She laughed and said, "It's wonderful, isn't it?"

"Sure. If you want to bathe in public. In the middle of Main Street. While listening to Christmas music."

Still laughing, Mary said, "All right, Grinch. Not the real thing. But still, you don't have to freeze your bottom off. Nor do you have to scrap ice off your windshield. And if you want to go swimming tomorrow, you can."

Remembering his unplanned dip in her father's pool, he smirked at her but still said, "Okay. I'll concede those points."

"Hey, Mary. Turn this way and smile," Mac called out, pointing a camera in their direction.

Mary obeyed and Trevor couldn't help to grin at her enthusiasm. Then was surprised when Mac said, "Trevor. Get in closer. Let me get you in the frame."

His arm went automatically around Mary and they smiled at the photographer as the "snow" whirled around them. Okay, he would admit, it was sorta fun. And silly.

He laughed as he looked around, enjoying the joy on everyone's faces. It was magical.

"See. Not bad for Florida, huh?"

"I suppose so," Trevor said, turning to Mary. He chuckled when he noticed soap flakes clinging to Mary's eyelashes. "Hold on." His hand went to her shoulder to hold her gently as his other hand wiped the flakes from her face. He took his time doing this as he studied her face.

And he didn't want to let go. He frowned, not liking the feeling at all. Her eyes looked up at him, wide and innocent. Before he could censor himself, he muttered, "There's nothing going on between your mother and me."

Like a little kitten, she blinked twice. "What?"

The hand that removed the snow now went to her cheek to gently cup it. Trevor enjoyed the soft feel of her skin. His blood heated as he caressed her face. His heart thumped as his eyes met hers and held. He wanted to tell her he was just as confused as she.

Instead, he took her upper arms in both of his hands. "Your mother and I are only business associates. Nothing more is going on between us."

Mary stared for another moment and then as if waking from a dream, she shook her head. "I don't understand. All that 'darling' and 'I want Merrilyn to have a good Christmas.' Now you tell me nothing's going on?"

She shook his hands off her and started back to the parade sign-up table but he quickly caught up with her.

Trevor followed her, running his fingers through his hair in frustration. "Come on. If you'll think back, it was Merrilyn using the endearments, which she does with everyone. And I do want her to have a good Christmas. She's been a very good employer to me. Nothing more."

Merrilyn sat at the sign-up table and smiled when they approached. "Mary. It's been really slow. Everyone's more interested in the ah . . . snow."

"Merrilyn. Would you tell your daughter that we are merely business associates, nothing more?"

She glanced at Trevor, Mary, and back to him. To his horror, she winked and said, "Oh, of course, darling. Just associates." To make matters worse, she grinned. Smugly.

"Merrilyn!"

Trevor saw Mary's expression fall. Her shoulders hunched. Her voice lowered as she said, "You can leave now, Mom. I'll take over the table. Besides, Brad will be here soon."

"Mary, no. It's not—"

"Oh, would you look there," Merrilyn said. "It's Harriet Wingate. I need to go say hello to her. She's an important contact in town. Come with me, Trevor dear. You need to meet her."

Trevor couldn't understand this, but he definitely did not like it. Seeing that Mary was closed up, already speaking with others, he followed Merrilyn. And sighed heavily. Something was going on here and he did not like being in the middle of it.

Nor would he be, for long.

Chapter Seven

Mary shuffled to her door early the next morning to answer a knock. She was ready to slam the door on whoever was interrupting her last few minutes of sleep.

It had been an interminable night, with little rest.

She was tired, cranky, and angry when she pulled open the door to reveal Trevor standing there, looking fresh as the proverbial daisy.

"What . . . what are you doing here?" Mary hid behind the door so he wouldn't notice her sleeping attire of faded extra-large tee shirt and baggy sweatpants.

"I'm sorry to bother you." She really didn't think he was. "Could I come in for a few minutes?"

Mary glanced at the clock on the wall. She wiped the remaining sleep out of her eyes and gave one last yawn. "Why are you here at six thirty in the morning? At my apartment? You couldn't wait to torment me at a decent hour?"

Trevor pushed the door slightly so that he could enter, which he did. Mary followed his eyes and was grateful that she'd straightened up yesterday morning. She watched him turn to her and when he didn't wince at her appearance decided that she'd at least hear what he had to say. Then she'd kick him out.

"I know. Again, I'm sorry."

The intensity of Trevor's eyes had Mary frowning. "What's wrong?"

His eyes showed agitation, like a field of bright grass being bullied by a stubborn wind. He stepped closer to her. "I am not having an affair with your mother."

The words affair and mother spoken together in one sentence sent a deep pain through her heart. "Okay. Whatever you say."

"And I'm going to prove it to you."

Mary's head cocked. "How?"

"I'm meeting Merrilyn for some coffee in the kitchen. I want you to stand outside the door and listen. I'll get her to speak the truth about our relationship."

A glimmer of hope blossomed in Mary as she thought perhaps Trevor might be telling the truth. Before she could dwell on that, she again frowned. "Why? Why is this so important to prove to me?"

The expression on Trevor's face surprised Mary, as the man was actually speechless with the question.

"I . . . ah, don't exactly know. I guess I just want you to know the truth."

That wasn't it, Mary was sure. But she didn't want to take the time to find out his real motives. What she did want was to know about her mother and what was really going on. Besides helping her with the parade, which was a flimsy excuse to begin with, why was she here in Charity and why did she bring Trevor?

Her voice emotionless, she said, "Give me three minutes to change."

Trevor had been honest when he told Mary he wasn't sure why he was at her apartment early in the morning to prove that he wasn't involved with Merrilyn. Maybe he didn't want her to think he was some gigolo, romancing a much older woman. Maybe it was for his own sanity. Either way, he wanted the truth to come out.

When Mary returned a few minutes later in jeans and a light blue sweater, he couldn't help smiling. With her hair pulled back in a ponytail, she looked like a teenager. A very sweet teenager. He quickly pulled his eyes away from her and said, "Come on."

"There you are, darling," Merrilyn said as she poured herself a cup of coffee in the Swenson kitchen. "I hope you like strong coffee. It's too early for Elena and I wasn't quite sure how to use this old coffee maker."

"I'm sure it's fine." Trevor joined her, getting his own coffee.

They each took a sip and then Merrilyn said, "All right, tell me what's bothering you. You said it was urgent."

"Yes." Trevor put his cup on the counter and leaning against it, folded his arms across his chest. "I'd like for you to tell me why you want everyone to think that you and I are a couple."

Merrilyn's chuckles had him clenching his molars. "Is that all? Really darling, I could have used another couple of hours of beauty sleep."

"What are you trying to pull? I'm getting death stares from everyone here—the people in town, your daughter, your *husband*." Trevor thought he saw a momentary smile on Merrilyn's face before it disappeared. "I really don't like being the bad guy in this scenario."

"You sound like it's a terrible rumor. Am I that old and unattractive?"

Trevor emitted a groan of frustration. "Merrilyn, don't veer off the issue. You're an excellent boss. Extremely intelligent and considerate. But I don't think you're being fair to me with this pretense." Trevor cautiously peered back to make sure that Mary was still standing outside the room.

Merrilyn patted his hand and then took her coffee to the small breakfast table. "Perhaps you're right, Trevor. I have . . . allowed everyone to believe what they will about us," she said gesturing with her hand as if the matter was of no consequence. "People are going to gossip no matter what, you know that. What do you want me to do?"

"I know that people will believe whatever they want. But . . ." His voice growing a little louder, Trevor said, "I'd like for you to tell your daughter and your husband in no ambiguous terms that you and I are not, nor have we ever been, romantically involved."

Merrilyn gave a pout. "You really want me to do that?"

Trevor sighed dramatically. He knew that Mary could very well interpret Merrilyn's tone in a host of different ways. He'd try another tactic. "Mrs. Kennedy Swenson. Have we ever been intimate with each other?"

Merrilyn laughed and said, "You really did wake up saucy today." He frowned and she gave her own sigh. "No. Never."

"Has there ever been any romantic leaning between us since we first began working together?"

Merrilyn took his hand in hers and said, "Of course not. Trevor, you are my right arm. Why would I threaten that with a romantic liaison?"

"Then why are you parading him around as if he were your own boy toy?" Mary called out, coming into the kitchen.

Merrilyn dropped Trevor's hand, her face tightening and her lips thinning. "Mary."

"Why, Mom? I'd like an answer to my question." Mary stood in the kitchen her hands fisted at her sides.

Trevor folded his arms in eager anticipation as he too wanted an answer.

Merrilyn tried to answer. It was amazing to watch the usually confident woman search for an answer. "I . . . I, well, I guess I just wanted everyone to believe that I was . . . still beautiful, still desirable."

"Mom." Mary's hands went to the side of her head as if to shut out the noise coming from her mother. "First . . . euwww! Second, why was that even important to you to begin with?"

"Don't you know why, Mary?"

Trevor turned to see Frank coming into the kitchen. As they waited, he casually pulled out a mug and filled it with coffee. He took a moment to take a long sip of the hot brew.

"Your mother here, for some strange reason, wanted to try to make me jealous."

Merrilyn's face scrunched, instantly turning all different shades of red. "Jealous. Is that what you think?"

"I know you, Merry. I know how that twisted mind of yours works. You get an idea in your head and then you work it like an old dog with a bone." Trevor hid the grin when Merrilyn gasped. "You'd like nothing else than to have me crazy with jealousy, begging you to please come back to me. But I'm not jealous and do you know why?"

The room was stunned into silence.

"Because only a fool would believe that a young, intelligent man here like Trevor would take up with a fifty-five-year-old mother of a beautiful daughter his own age."

Trevor decided that he liked Frank Swenson.

"I'm not fifty-five," Merrilyn returned quietly.

Frank shrugged. "Close enough. You should be ashamed of yourself. Why, you scared Mary half to death."

"But not you," Merrilyn said, her tone flat, along with her eyes.

Frank had the audacity to laugh. He laughed loud and long. Trevor saw the surprise in Mary's eyes and the fury in Merrilyn's. The tension grew heavy. Maybe if he simply backed up, he could escape the family drama.

"But Dad, you were so insistent on Trevor staying at a hotel."

"Mainly because of you. I had no idea what kind of character Merry was bringing into our house. He could have been a serial killer for all we knew." He took a deep sip of his coffee.

"Perhaps my intention of coming to Charity had nothing to do with making you jealous. Sweetheart," Merrilyn said. Her voice was low and cool, with a knifed edge that Trevor had never heard before. "Perhaps I felt it was time to offer my daughter the opportunity of a lifetime. A chance to make a name for herself in the big city. Taking over my business."

Trevor's head snapped toward Merrilyn. Had he heard right? Couldn't be. He almost choked as he said, "What?"

Frank took a step to Merrilyn. "And why do you think Mary would leave home to go to some loud, obnoxious city to plan parties for the rich and arrogant? Especially when she'll have my land development business to run in a few more years."

Trevor tried to control the surprise, hurt, and anger that was balling in the pit of his stomach. "You're going to give your daughter the events business? Kennedy Swenson Events? Her? Just give it to her?"

Merrilyn ignored him and stood, her eyes staying on her husband. "You're . . . Are you kidding me? Why should she want to get her hands dirty in the building business when she can do great things in New York?"

"By planning parties?"

"Yes, by planning parties. Great things are done at parties—networking, transactions, humanitarian projects. All in a very civilized and elegant environment."

"The same could be done by a phone call!"

Merrilyn gasped. "You take that back!"

"Not on your life!"

"Mary's going with me!"

"She's staying with me!"

"Stop! Both of you stop!"

Trevor turned to see a saddened Mary wearily standing by the sink.

"Mother. You've never said anything to me about taking over your business." She looked at Frank. "Dad. I've never given you any indication that I wanted to take over yours. What is wrong with you people?"

Trevor would have loved to chime in to answer that one but wisely kept his mouth shut. Especially as he saw the distraught expression on Mary's face.

"I can't please the both of you. What do you want from me? I feel like a ball being batted back and forth between you two, and it hurts. Now, I love you both, but you've got to stop making me the spoils of your battles."

Trevor approved of her commentary. Now she should go in for the kill, in his opinion, and excuse herself, suggesting they actually discuss their relationship with each other.

He was sorely disappointed when she inserted herself in the solution by saying, "If you two would like to sit down, I'm sure we can work all this out. It could be the start of a wonderful Christmas season, don't you think?"

Trevor closed his eyes and sighed.

"I have a better idea," Frank said to his daughter. "How about I take you out for breakfast. You can make sure I don't get something loaded with too much fat." He took his daughter's arm and led her out, with Mary giving her mother a sad glance.

Frank couldn't help giving Merrilyn one last dig. "Coffee's okay. Although Mrs. Appleby makes it much better."

Trevor took a breath to try to calm the fury he was feeling for the two Swenson women. For Mary with an "a" one "r," because she wouldn't leave her parents alone to work out their problems. And for Merrilyn—what had she been thinking? How could she have just offered Mary *his* position, the one he'd been working so hard for, the one Merrilyn had practically promised him? If

Mary was taking over, he was leaving on the first flight back to New York.

He'd have to find another way to help his family.

As he tried to form words that wouldn't turn the air blue, he faced Merrilyn and the rant froze on his tongue. She looked so vulnerable, so hurt. So fragile that a stiff wind would have knocked her over. Trevor's compassionate side surfaced. She had been good to him, a good employer and friend. His conscience wouldn't let him verbally tear her apart like he wanted to. "You okay?" he asked quietly.

Tears filled her eyes as she gave a delicate shrug.

Growing up in a large household that included a mom and four sisters, he knew when words were not needed. Only comfort. So he put his own anger aside for the moment and walked to Merrilyn, putting his arm around her. Her head went to his side as she wept.

A couple of minutes later, she walked to the counter and pulled out a paper towel to wipe her eyes. "Trevor, why don't we go over the contracts for the first of the year."

"I've got them in my briefcase," he said.

As he headed out of the room, he thought, fine. They'd work on contracts. *But we are going to have a conversation about the future of this company, Merrilyn.*

Chapter Eight

"It won't be long, honey. Just a week, maybe ten days."

"But Mac, it's the Christmas season. There's so much going on here in Charity. You'll miss it all."

"I won't. Now give me a kiss before I go pack."

Grace McCrae went willingly into her husband's arms and held him tight. Since the massive success of *Christmas In America*, Mac's beautiful coffee table book, the offers for other assignments had been pouring in for the famous photographer. He'd declined the vast majority of them, she knew, because he wanted to spend his time in the small town with her.

But his agent was working on a contract for a new four book deal showcasing each season in America. They were still in negotiations with the publishers, but Grace knew how bad Mac wanted this. She also knew that she should be supportive and loving in his decision to travel for most of the next year.

She was miserable thinking of the next year.

They embraced and her lips eagerly sought his. Her arms circled his neck and she pulled him closer. There was nowhere on earth she wanted to be. They kissed again and again and were both breathless when surfacing for air.

"Grace. Baby, you're making it so hard to leave." Mac went back to her lips his hands running down her sides.

The clock sitting on their foyer table chimed the hour, causing Mac to back away. "I really have to get ready," he whispered, giving her a small smile.

She tried to return the smile as Mac disappeared upstairs. Grace looked around the Victorian home that Mary had helped them find in the heart of downtown Charity. It was perfect for them and they'd enjoyed decorating it to fit their style.

Grace looked around the family room. Amidst the comfy furniture were framed photographs from Mac's collection. Several were pictures of her, lovingly composed by Mac. Stunning photos of Charity dominated one wall.

Then there were their wedding pictures. Grace's heart swelled with happiness, as it always did, when she viewed those pictures. It had been about two years since she'd met and fallen in love with Mac. He had quite simply revolutionized her world. She loved him so much.

When the phone rang, she called out, "I've got it," and picked it up.

"Grace? Are you busy for lunch? I really need someone to talk to."

"Mary. Is something wrong?"

"I just need to vent. How about it? I could grab some sandwiches and come over."

Mac returned with his duffel packed.

"Sure. Sounds great. See you soon." Grace hung up and gave her husband a hug. "You'll be back in time for the school kids coming by Hal's Place to see Santa, right?"

Mac kissed her head. "Of course. How could I possibly miss that?" With one finger under her chin, he lifted her head. "That was one of our first kisses, as I remember," he whispered and then proceeded to kiss her deeply.

Grace sighed. "Have a safe trip."

"I will. Be back before you know it." He hesitated and then said, "This is such a big opportunity, Grace. You know that, right?" She nodded.

And then he was gone. Grace looked at the foyer clock wondering when Mary would get there. She had some venting to do herself.

Mary felt much better after lunch with Grace. She'd told her everything and appreciated her objective outlook. Then had listened as Grace poured out her concerns about Mac's new career opportunities.

To keep themselves from getting totally depressed, they talked about the big romance in town—Big Jed and Elena. At the town's decorating party, he'd escorted the woman around as if she were the queen of England. Mary and Grace giggled at how Big Jed had introduced her to every adult, child, and dog in attendance. And when they'd danced in the snow . . . Both women sighed. It was so sweet.

The midday break had helped Mary get her perspective back. And prepare for the invitation from her mother to go shopping after work. She'd declined at first, but when Merrilyn suggested they might discuss a few ideas for the parade, she agreed. The time was going by quickly and she did need to work on the stupid parade.

For some reason, no one seemed to be signing up. If she didn't get busy, the big event would consist of a float from Hal's Place and Big Jed in a sleigh pulled by her and her mother in dolphin costumes. Not good.

The Millennia Mall was their destination, a two-story shopping center that boasted the most upscale shops in Central Florida. Mary drove, their conversation staying on neutral subjects such as the weather, Christmas, and plans for the parade.

After shopping for a few hours, they had dinner at The Cheesecake Factory. The time together was comfortable, as Mary knew that her mother was trying to establish the peace between them and she was all for that.

After splitting a piece of Oreo Cookie Cheesecake, they walked the mall, hoping to burn off the extra million calories. Mary felt at ease to share her frustrations. "I don't understand why I'm having such a hard time getting businesses and organizations to sign up for the parade."

"That's not uncommon. I run into it all the time. Christmas is a busy time anyway. People cringe when you want to add something else."

"I don't blame them." Mary groaned. "I wish I hadn't come up with the idea in the first place."

Mary put her arm around her daughter. "Now, honey, it was a good idea. The trick is like with all marketing. You simply have to show the person how the idea will benefit them."

"I get it, but I don't have time for all that. To do this thing right, I need a theme, I need flyers, incentives, packets with easy instructions. I've got three closings in the next two weeks."

"How about if I work on the flyers and packets and Trevor hits the street to get sign-ups."

"Don't you two have your own work?"

"Yes, we do. But everything's under control." She squeezed Mary into her side. "After all, this is why I'm here. To help you. Oh, let's stop and watch the kids see Santa. For just a couple of minutes."

They stood near a rail on the second story and looked down at the spectacular North Pole wonderland created for children to meet Santa. The line was long, filled with excited kids and anxious parents.

Merrilyn chuckled. "I remember bringing you to see Santa when you were a child. You were never that excited. You were . . . analytical, I'd guess."

"What do you mean?"

"To you Christmas was a puzzle. You didn't understand it and you weren't really sure about the Santa stuff." She grinned. "But you wanted to talk to him just in case."

Mary laughed. "I suppose I was just covering my bases."

"Yes. And you wanted to please us, knowing how excited we were about the season." Merrilyn smiled. "Your dad and I always wanted you to have the best of Christmases." Merrilyn's hand went to her mouth to cover a laugh. "I remember one Christmas in particular. Your father was up until three in the morning putting together that bicycle built for two. Then the next morning after you'd seen it, he remembered that he'd left the horn and the basket in the garage. He had a hard time trying to figure out how to get those things to you." She giggled at the memory. "Finally, he had me take you to the kitchen to make pancakes so he could sneak out, wrap those things, and bring them in."

"I remember," Mary said, smiling. "I wondered where those gifts had come from."

"Your father was so concerned that you'd be suspicious. But I told him not to worry about it. Just enjoy the day with the family."

The realization that they weren't a family anymore caused a silence between them. Mary went back to gazing at the children with their parents and visiting Santa. She felt so sad.

"So, when are you seeing Brad next?" Merrilyn asked.

Mary was a little surprised by the question, but said, "Oh, we're planning to see the Nutcracker downtown."

"Splendid. I'd love to see the Nutcracker. And I think your father should spend more time with Brad if the two of you are dating. I'll have Trevor get four tickets—You, Brad, your father, and me. Sound good?"

The mention of her assistant's name brought conflicting emotions. Mary was glad that he'd insisted on having her mother admit the truth about their relationship. And there had been a few moments when they'd looked at each other and the attraction had been off the charts.

But he'd been avoiding her since that awful incident in her parents' kitchen. Thinking back, he had seemed distracted when her parents had argued. Maybe he was embarrassed to have witnessed the scene. She'd been more than embarrassed he'd seen her family at their worst.

Mary saw her mother's hopeful expression and said, "Okay, sure."

They both went back to watching the kids. "I'm not going to New York with you, Mom." She hadn't meant to just blurt that out but it had to be said.

"Just think about it, honey. No reason to make a decision just now."

Mary faced her mother and said, "I feel like I'm a possession that you and Dad are fighting over. I don't like that feeling."

"I know, dear." Merrilyn's eyes shone with unshed tears as they stayed on the Christmas scene below.

"What happened, Mom?" Mary whispered. "It's been five years and you two haven't spoken. Haven't even seen each other. Why?"

"That's better left alone, Mary."

"Not if I'm in the middle of it. Why can't the three of us sit down and work through whatever happened? Can't you see? You both are unhappy, living in a kind of limbo."

"I'm not . . ." Merrilyn faced the rail again. "I'm not living in limbo. And your father and I will deal with this. In our own time. In our own way."

Mary studied her mother. Merrilyn Kennedy Swenson had always been a drama queen, able to conjure up any emotion needed for the moment. But right now her face showed a sadness that Mary had never seen before. Her eyes were constantly blinking, trying to hold back tears, real ones. Her lips were trembling so that Merrilyn bit her lower lip to still them. Mary noticed that her perfect posture had slightly slumped and her knuckles were gripping the rail as if her life depended on it.

This was no act. Her mother really was devastated.

And Mary wanted to comfort her, just as her mother had comforted her so many times as a child. She moved closer and put her arm around Merrilyn, pulling her close. As her own eyes teared up, she said, "I love you, Mom."

"I love you too, honey," Merrilyn whispered.

They stood like that for a long time watching the children below. Ideas began to fly through Mary's head. Why would her mother be so upset if she didn't still care at least a little for her husband? Her mother had never pursued a divorce. She'd never been interested in another man. Her father had never pursued a divorce or another woman. Could there possibly be hope for her parents' marriage? Maybe if she could get them together, get them to spend time with each other they could rekindle their romance.

And the first step would be to get them together on a date. To the Nutcracker Suite.

"What do you mean you can't make it to the Nutcracker? You've got a ticket!"

"That's all right, honey. I'm sure Trevor can go in my place," Frank said with a hint of sarcasm.

Mary was scrambling now. This was not the plan. She'd already organized everything in her mind. Her parents would sit together. They'd be caught up in the music. He'd take her hand and look into her eyes and she'd blush slightly.

Okay, Merrilyn blushing was a little out there but Mary could dream.

And now her dad was blowing the whole romantic scheme because he had a dinner meeting he *said* he couldn't get out of.

Frank kissed Mary's head. "You'll probably have a better time without me anyway. Remember, I fell asleep last year when you dragged me to it."

But now she was going to have to spend the evening with Brad, her mother, and (gulp) Trevor. She was already starting to squirm.

When her doorbell rang at six o'clock on the dot, her mind rushed back to the evening at hand. And her date.

"Brad. Come on in." She pulled him by the hand into her small apartment. Maybe she should think more seriously about Brad. Was there a chance of a relationship other than friends between them?

"Good evening, Mary. You look nice." He took his glasses off and pulling a handkerchief from his pocket started to clean them. "Thank you for inviting me tonight."

"You're welcome. Although there has been a change of plans. My dad won't be joining us."

"Nothing wrong, I hope."

"No, schedule conflict. So Trevor will be taking his place. Have you met him?"

"Oh, you mean your mother's . . . ah, no, I don't believe I have."

She shouldn't be irritated. Brad was merely thinking what everyone in town was probably thinking. She sighed and grabbed her purse. "Well, let's go."

It was just one evening. She could endure one evening with . . .

Oh. My. Gosh. Mary watched as Trevor escorted her mother to the hired limo. Why did the guy continue to increase in good looks? *He'll probably be a calendar pinup when he's in his nineties.*

Trevor wore a navy suit with a white shirt and a blue, turquoise, and aqua striped tie. The colors caused the green in his eyes to intensify, creating an incredible package.

She'd have to keep from looking at his eyes.

Mary quickly turned to Brad to remember what *her* date was wearing. Black suit, black tie, white shirt, black glasses. Easy to remember but hardly memorable.

Still, she gave Brad a smile and adjusted his tie before gathering her nerve to greet the others.

"You must be Brad. I'm Trevor Crane." Trevor smiled, his hand extended.

Brad shook, polite as ever. "Nice to meet you, Trevor. Welcome to Charity."

"Thank you." Trevor gave a polite but cool nod to Mary. "Good evening."

"Good evening." She figured Trevor was still embarrassed by witnessing the horrible argument between her parents. She couldn't blame him.

After Brad was introduced to her mother, they headed over to the limo. A hand went to Mary's back to steady her and she felt a bolt of lightning surge through her body. At first she'd thought it was Brad, but looking back saw that he'd stepped to the side to take a call. Her eyes went to Trevor who assisted her into the car. She quickly got settled, as far away from Trevor Crane as possible.

Why did she have to wear her hair up? It only highlighted a slender and graceful neck that Trevor yearned to nibble on.

106

She was muddling up all his plans. After the initial shock of learning that Merrilyn was going to give the company to Mary, Trevor was confused. What should he do? He needed this job, needed the yearly bonus. So, after thinking it through, he'd determined the right thing was to calm down and monitor the situation instead of just hightailing it back to New York.

Still, he couldn't help the feeling of betrayal that Merrilyn would give his job to her daughter. And speaking of Mary, with an "a" one "r." Obviously, this job offer made it impossible to act upon the attraction between them.

Then she had to go and wear her hair up. And sit with him in an enclosed car, where the scent of her subtle perfume curled into his nostrils as a haunting lure from a mystic siren.

He had to remember that she was with a date, the nerdy but polite scientist Brad. Trevor's presence was only to be a fourth person. He would be polite, talk about the weather, the Nutcracker, the parade. But he would not look into the blue eyes of his possibly future boss. Egad!

The evening went smoothly for the most part. Merrilyn was on her best behavior. She didn't overuse the word "darling" when speaking with Trevor and she didn't interrogate Brad. She was her usual charming self, for which Mary was thankful.

Trevor was another story. The man was constantly bothering her. Oh, not in any direct way. He asked Brad about his work, which was as dry as dust, but again demonstrated his diverse arenas of knowledge. He was courteous to her mother, the perfect date.

He was well mannered to Mary, never showing her more attention than was appropriate.

Merrilyn said something that made Trevor laugh and Mary's breath caught at the way his laughter transformed his face. Like a mischievous angel enjoying the moment, she thought. *Oh, yeah, he'll be a ninety-year old pinup for sure*. Trevor turned and seeing her staring at him, grinned, almost as if he knew what she was thinking.

When the limo dropped them off back at the Swenson home close to eleven, Brad expressed his thanks and quickly left, citing an early morning meeting. Merrilyn also left, yawning and citing an evening meeting—with her bed.

That left Mary and Trevor alone in the darkened driveway.

There was a fog of tension that seemed to surround them, making Mary uncomfortable. As she was about to excuse herself, Trevor said, "Do you have a few minutes? I'd like to talk to you."

"I, ah, don't know. It's kinda late."

"It's important. Mary." He smiled slightly. "The parade. Remember?" His eyes were intent in the lone light shining over the front door. Mary wavered with her reply until he said, "It's the least you can do since we're not going to become stepfather and daughter after all."

The mirth in his expression was too much for her. She chuckled and said, "All right. How about a cup of coffee?"

"Great." He put his hand to her back once more and the physical awareness threatened to overwhelm her. As she led him up the staircase to her garage apartment, she wondered.

Was she going to regret this?

Chapter Nine

Trevor knew it was probably a mistake. He should be patient, but he had to know if she was leaning one way or the other in the decision to take over her mother's company. They'd had an enjoyable evening, surely they could have a civil discussion about the future of Kennedy Swenson Events. Just to get a gauge one way or the other.

Mary let him inside her small apartment and said, "I'm get your coffee. Just make yourself at home."

"Thanks." He glanced around, something he had not done on the morning he'd been there. The apartment was compact but colorful and inviting. The walls were white with bright abstract paintings adding life. The upholstered furniture was a mix of whites, creams, and beiges but was made interesting by pillows in blues, reds, and purples. If he didn't know any better, he could have been in a tasteful flat in Manhattan. He was impressed.

"I didn't know if you wanted sugar or cream so I brought both." Mary returned from the kitchen and set a tray down on the coffee table.

Trevor watched her, noticing the grace and competence she exhibited in doing such a mundane chore. When she straightened, catching him staring at her, she blushed.

When was the last time he'd seen a woman blush? It was really quite lovely.

"Shall we sit?" he said motioning to the loveseat.

"Of course." Mary sat and took her cup of coffee, adding just a touch of cream. "So, you wanted to talk?"

He joined her on the loveseat. As casually as he knew how, he said, "I just wondered if you'd made any decisions concerning taking over your mother's business."

Mary huffed out a breath and sat back against the cushions. "Trevor, I cannot apologize enough for the actions of my parents the other day."

He shrugged. "They were worked up. It happens to the best of us. So, have you—"

"I was mortified. And shocked, to say the least."

"I guess so. But have you thought—"

"But if anything good came out of it, I think it was the fact that they still have very deep feelings for one another."

"Okay. So, are you . . . what?"

"They wouldn't have argued so vehemently if they didn't care. Maybe there's still hope for their marriage after all."

As Mary took a sip, Trevor held his tongue. How could they possibly have a chance if all they did was bicker and fight? But he knew she didn't want to hear that. Returning to his main objective, he said, "So, taking over your mother's company still a possibility?"

"Oh, I don't know. Probably not. I mean, it's a great company, a great opportunity, but really, I'm happy doing what I'm doing."

Trevor let out a deep breath. *Thank God*, was all he could think.

"Now, what were you thinking about the parade? You have ideas?" Her bright eyes sparkled.

Suddenly, the future seemed a little brighter. *Oh, yeah. I've got ideas*. When Mary continued to look at him, obviously waiting for an answer, he said, "Yeah, the parade. I think the key lies with your theme. You need a good theme that will excite the community, get them involved."

He added cream to his coffee and sitting back took a sip. "I understand the parade is an effort to provide the annual tourists with another slice of Charity." Mary nodded. "Then I say, make the theme of the parade 'Proud to be Charity.' Emphasize to the town that this is their opportunity to show the world that Charity is the best small town in the country. Especially at Christmas."

He could see that she was thinking, warming up to the idea.

"Showcase and celebrate a Charity Christmas. Who wouldn't love to be part of that?" Mary glanced at him, very much impressed. "How did you come up with this?"

Trevor felt somewhat embarrassed when he said, "I went by Hal's Place. Bought one of those books *Christmas in America*. Charity had a big spread. Although I love New York, I could see how people would be drawn to it." He saw the smug grin that Mary was trying to hide. "Yes, even big city boy here can appreciate the best of a small town."

She chuckled and Trevor felt his heart thud against his chest. If she didn't stop being so appealing, he was going to have to bolt before he did something stupid.

"So, you're human. Good to know. And I like that idea, a lot." Mary sighed. "I just wish I had more time to do this properly."

Trevor set his cup down and reached over to take her hand in a friendly gesture. "I'll do a bit of research tomorrow. Merrilyn can put a brochure and packet together and then if you can swing a couple of hours, you and I will canvas the town. We'll get all the sign-ups you need."

Mary's eyes twinkled. Her smile was dazzling. She set her cup down and took both his hands in hers. "Thank you. Thank you so much."

Trevor was about undone. Her small hands in his did strange things to his heart, which was now pounding. He gently caressed her hands, enjoying their softness. His eyes met hers and held as he gazed at the deep blue depths staring at him.

He had to kiss her, there was no question. But first he had to make sure of something.

In a voice low and roughened with need he said, "It's not serious between you and Brad, is it?"

"No," she whispered, her eyes staying on him.

"Thank God." His hands went gently to her shoulders and pulled her to him. He leaned into her until his lips touched hers, lightly, enjoying that first contact, letting the current of desire flow through his body. He pressed slightly harder, allowing his lips to move over hers and felt her soften against him. His fingers on her shoulder caressed, enjoying her slight purr. A feeling of protection and possessiveness welled up in him, so strong, so complete that he was taken aback.

A warning bell sounded in the back of his conscience. Yes, he'd initiated the kiss, wanted it. But he needed to be careful. He was only here for a season and then would be heading north.

He eased back and smiled at her, trying not to notice her bright eyes, her soft lips. "Well," he said.

"Well," she repeated.

"I, ah, guess I'd better get going. I'll give you a call when I've got everything together and we can set up a time to go canvassing." He gave her another smile. "Okay?"

She returned the smile and said, "That sounds good."

He quickly left, eager to regain control of his emotions. There was too much at stake to let a simple attraction blow out of proportion. And that's all it was, he kept telling himself.

"Mom? How are you? How's everyone doing?"

Trevor needed a little grounding. He hadn't been able to think of anything except that kiss since it had happened the night before. He was too distracted, so while Merrilyn went to the printers to get the brochures and packets for the parade printed up, Trevor took the time to call home.

"Trevor? Honey, it's so good to hear your voice. We're fine. Your father's feeling good today. I'm trying to keep him from overdoing it in the store. How are you, everything good?"

"Yeah, Mom. Everything's good." He smiled. There was always something about hearing his mother's voice that calmed him. "Merrilyn's got me helping out with a parade in this little town. It's really cute, you'd love it. I'm sending you a book with photographs of it by Stuart McCrae."

"I'm sure I'll love it."

"We had Thanksgiving at a little diner in town. It was closed but we were invited to meet others there for dinner. And afterwards there was a football game at one of the parks." He rubbed his bottom, where he had fallen several times that day. "I think I'm getting too old to play."

His mother laughed. "Never."

Trevor chuckled. "You won't believe it, but they actually have what they call snow on their main street. It's really soap bubbles but everyone gets so excited you'd think it was the real thing."

"Sounds like fun."

"And last night we went to see 'The Nutcracker.' I think that was probably my first time watching the whole show."

"Must have been good."

Something in his mother's tone stopped him. "Mom? Is something wrong?"

"No. Just thinking. You've never been such a big fan of Christmas. I remember when you were a child you spent more time sweeping the floors of the shop and organizing the shelves than you did pouring over the Christmas catalogs."

Trevor frowned. "That's because there was work to do."

"Yes, I know. But you just never seemed to get into it the way your brothers and sisters did. I wonder what has you so interested now."

Trevor said nothing. Mothers seemed to have a sixth sense when it came to their children and he didn't want to give her any help.

"There's a girl!" his mother gasped.

Too late.

"I . . . I . . . no, I wouldn't exactly say that."

"Trevor Crane, you always stutter when you don't want to admit I'm right. Now I want to know immediately, who is she?"

He sighed heavily. Maybe subconsciously he wanted to talk about Mary with his mother. God knew he needed help putting things in perspective.

"I . . . wouldn't exactly put too much stock in this, but there is someone."

"I knew it, I—"

"Mom, please. We're just, you know, merely acquaintances working toward being friends at this point. A long way from a serious relationship."

There was a brief hesitation before his mother said, "Well, what's taking you so long?"

Trevor couldn't help grinning. "Because it's a little more complicated than simply 'boy meets girl.'"

"Oh, pooh. How is it complicated? She has the good sense to be interested in you, doesn't she? And if she doesn't she isn't worth your time."

He chuckled. "It happens to be Merrilyn's daughter. Her name's Mary." *Mary with an "a" one "r,"* he thought with affection.

His mother hesitated before answering. "Merrilyn's little girl?"

"Merrilyn led me to believe Mary was a child but she's my age, probably a year or two younger."

"Oh, thank God. You realize I almost had a heart attack. What do you want to do, kill you poor old mother?" Mrs. Crane took a breath and said, "So what's the problem?"

Trevor blinked. "Didn't you hear what I said? It's my boss's daughter." He didn't add that the daughter might be taking over the company. She might actually become his boss.

"I can't see the problem. If you both have feelings for each other, you're both single, you can work out the rest."

"But I'll be back in New York in a few short weeks and she'll be here. How does that work?"

"Sweetheart. If love develops between the two of you, it's worth fighting for, worth making compromises. Believe me, when you find the right one, nothing is more important."

Trevor felt a warmth spread through his body. He knew how much his parents loved each other. They'd been through hard times, lean times, miserable times, but they always had the love for each other to pull them through. It was something he hoped to have someday.

His mother was right. He'd never know if he didn't pursue what was going on between them.

"Thanks, Mom. You always know how to make me feel better."

"So, you'll be here for New Years?"

"That's the plan. I'll keep you posted."

"Yes, keep me posted about your plans . . . and about Mary."

"And then we have the Senior Saints on their motorcycles attached to the sleigh and pulling it through the parade route," Big Jed said with a flourish.

Mary's wide eyes blinked twice. "Ah, I'm not sure what to say."

"Tell him what you think, Mary," Tom, the evening cook at Hal's Place who was pulling a double shift, said as he headed into the kitchen. "Crazy."

After the breakfast rush, Hal's place was usually pretty peaceful. And a haven for Mary as she needed a place to think. But today the haven would be short-lived as the annual holiday field trips of the schoolchildren to the diner would begin, where they'd be treated to Christmas cookies and milk, stories from waitress Joy, and a visit from Santa Claus.

Two other waitresses were on board today and joined Joy in hurrying around the dining room, getting ready for the onslaught of happy, excited children.

But Mary's mind wasn't noticing the bustle around her. Her lips still tingled from the kiss Trevor had given her two days before. She'd been kissed plenty of times. Plenty of times, she told herself. How could one little meeting of lips cause her world to completely come unglued? So there she sat with her fifth cup of coffee for the day trying to clue in to the world around her.

Big Jed's parade idea did the trick.

"It's not crazy, Tom," Big Jed said. "I think those bikers would get a kick out of pulling Santa, which happens to be me, through the parade."

"Didn't those bikers get ticketed just a month ago? Something about several members not wearing their glasses. One didn't have his hearing aid. They almost took out the 'Welcome to Charity' sign," Tom called out from the kitchen.

"Rumors. Besides, they just got a warning."

"I'll have to think about it, Big Jed," Mary said diplomatically.

"Hey, Mary," Grace said as she glided into the diner, a big smile on her face.

"You're chipper this morning. Ready for the deluge of munchkins today?"

Grace chuckled. "Yes, I am. Mac's plane should be landing in Orlando as we speak."

"In time for the kids, then," Big Jed commented.

"Of course." Grace went behind the counter and pulled out a clean apron. "He's got to be here as 'Santa' and pull out a sprig of mistletoe to give Miss Grace a kiss." She chuckled. "Mary, you want any breakfast before we shut down for the kids?"

"How can you stay here and eat when you've got that goddess at home preparing your meals, something that puts this place to shame," Big Jed said.

"Hey!" Tom and Grace said simultaneously.

"Sorry. No offense intended."

Mary laughed. "If you mean Elena, you're right that she's great. Her food is amazing." Seeing that Big Jed wanted more information, she grinned and said, "All right. What do you want to know?"

"Is Elena seeing someone special?"

She thought about that. "I really don't know. But I can't believe that she is, not the way she was looking at you last week." Big Jed sat up straight and smoothed the few hairs that lay over his bald head, causing Mary to giggle.

She quickly got serious. "But you know that she's here for just a few weeks, don't you? When Christmas is over she'll go with my mom back to New York."

"Pretty Mary, at my age you realize to live each day as it comes. And to not ignore the magic that happens between a man and a woman."

Mary felt her face heat up. Did he know about her feelings for Trevor? She'd been trying to downplay her emotions. Although her whole body was heating up just contemplating that magic that Jed spoke about.

"You okay, honey?" Big Jed asked.

"Oh, sure." She looked at Big Jed's happy face and leaned over to kiss his feathery cheek. "And I'm happy you're interested in Elena. I'll do anything to help the relationship."

"Hot dang. I like hearing that." He took a last sip of coffee and stood. "Think I'll head over and ask her to ride in the float with me. She could dress as Mrs. Santa."

Thankfully, he left before Mary let out a laugh.

"Hey, I wanted to let you know that I came up with an idea for Hal's Place in the parade," Grace said.

"Great. Shoot."

"A float."

Mary frowned. "Yeah, I know. A float."

"No, I mean we'll be a float."

"Yes, Grace, I know. You're going to have a float in the parade."

Grace burst out laughing. "No. I mean our float will be . . . a float. You know, an ice cream float. Get it?"

The rest of the diner broke into peals of laughter over the idea. Mary joined in, grateful for the lighthearted moment when she could let go of the heavier topics she had on her mind.

The moment was short lived when the door to the diner opened.

Chapter Ten

Trevor walked in, handsome as ever, carrying a pile of brochures and packets. When his eyes met Mary's, she felt her heart clench.

He stepped to the counter and dropped the papers down. "Here you go. I think Merrilyn did a great job."

Mary quickly looked through the papers, glad to have something other than Trevor's expressive eyes to concentrate on. "They look wonderful."

"Well, give me a packet so I can fill it out," Grace said, a smile on her face. "And be sure to leave a few of the brochures by the cash register. We'll help get the news out."

"I thought if you're not busy, we could walk the parade route. Think through any logistics that might be a problem for that day."

Mary looked up. Big mistake. "Okay," she whispered.

"Oh no. They're early," Grace cried. "Everyone, the first wave is coming!" A long line of smiling first graders was headed toward the restaurant, along with their diligent teachers and chaperones. Grace grabbed a damp rag to finish cleaning tables as she yelled instructions to everyone.

Mary jumped up and assisted, setting napkins at each place at the tables. Joy quickly started arranging plastic Christmas cups on trays to be filled with cold milk or water when the kids were seated.

"Can I do anything to help?" Trevor asked, watching the flurry of activity.

"Yeah. Could you help Tom in the kitchen? And send Dana and Lillian, the other waitresses, back in here to help with crowd control," Grace said, not looking up from her task.

"On it," Trevor said, moving into the kitchen.

Mary grinned. She was sure that Trevor hadn't signed on to help with a bunch of kids coming to see Santa. It was sweet of him to volunteer.

The kids were settled into seats and quieted down. Grace welcomed them to Hal's Place and made the mistake of asking them if they were ready for Christmas. The thunderous "yes" almost shook the photos off the wall. Mary giggled. They really were so cute.

Grace introduced Joy and the petite waitress began to regale the children with Christmas stories from her home country of France. Her gentle voice was hypnotic to the kids as they quieted and listened.

Grace grabbed Mary's arm and pulled her into the kitchen. "What are we going to do? Mac's not here yet!"

"Well, give him a call. See where he is?"

"Yes, of course." Grace fumbled out her phone and called Mac. "Where are you? The first group is here?" She listened as her expression dropped. "What?" Mary had a bad feeling as Grace's eyes filled. "Yeah, I know. Okay. See you then."

The kitchen was quiet as Tom, Trevor, and Mary watched her. Grace wiped away a stray tear before it could fall and said, "He's still on the tarmac in New York. Engine trouble. He hadn't been able to call." She sighed and said, "He's not going to make it today."

Mary moved to her side and put her arm around her friend. "There's nothing he can do about that. He'll get here as soon as he can."

"Yeah." Grace sniffed. "And in the meantime those kids out there are expecting a Santa. I don't want to disappoint them."

Mary's heart went out to her friend. She rubbed her arm and dropped her head against Grace's. Then having a thought said, "Is the costume in the office?"

Grace sniffed again and said, "Yes."

"Well . . . how about Tom putting on the costume and posing as Santa? That could work, right?"

Grace and Mary looked over at Tom, eyeing him. He turned red and replied, "Oh, no, I don't think so. I used all my 'ho, ho, ho's' with my own kids. Besides, Mac's shorter than me. The costume wouldn't fit."

"He's right," Grace said. Then as if thinking the same thing, Grace, Mary, and Tom all looked over at Trevor who was busy placing two cookies on each plate for the children.

Tom chuckled, "There you go."

Mary smiled widely. "That'll work."

Grace sighed. "I suppose we don't have a choice." She looked at the other two. "Let's do it."

Trevor didn't know how it happened. He'd just volunteered to help, trying to be a good Samaritan and now he was being suited up to play the part of Santa Claus to a bunch of sugar-infused youngsters.

Mary and Grace were sticking in the last pillow for his round belly, when Joy stuck her head in. "They are almost done with the cookies. Is he ready?"

"Give us a couple more minutes," Grace said standing back to look. "Can you get that zipper up, Mary? Now Trevor, you just 'ho, ho, ho' a lot when you go in. We'll have a seat for you and one by one the kids will sit on your lap. Ask them what they want for Christmas, yadda, yadda, yadda. Then before they go, give them a little candy cane. Got it?"

"Yeah, got it." Like he didn't know what Santa Claus did.

Grace took a breath and said, "I can never thank you enough, Trevor. Dinner's on me, okay."

"No problem." He gave her a grin and then she disappeared into the dining room.

Mary came in front of him and surveyed him from head to toe. Hands on her hips studying, she said, "Yes, I think you'll do."

"Oh, stop gushing." He grinned when Mary laughed. His heart lightened at the joy in her face. If this would make her happy, he'd suck it up and be the big guy for a while.

"It really is nice of you to help out, Trevor. This means so much to the children. And to Grace."

"Sure." Trevor was heating up and it wasn't because of the costume. Mary's eyes were a bright blue, shining at him. It was all he could do to keep from pulling her into his arms. Of course, the extra padding attached to his middle would make it a little difficult.

Still, he wanted her to know how he was feeling. "I hope you don't now associate me with a fat, old guy."

"No," she said with a chuckle. "Although, there is something to be said for a man who brings presents." She gave him a flirtatious smile and his temperature soared even higher.

He heard his cue, the children singing "Jingle Bells," and he gave a loud "Ho, ho, ho" as he left the office. His reception rivaled that of a rock star and he had no trouble smiling and playing the part.

"Well, has everyone been good this year?" he spoke in a deep, fatherly tone.

"Yes!" came the deafening reply.

"That's good because I have an extra big SUV sleigh that I'm carrying toys in this year." The kids giggled. "Rudolph and all the others have been working out with weights so they're ready." More giggles.

He settled down in the middle of the dining room and the teachers had one table at a time come forward to speak with him. Grace stood next to him with a large bag of candy canes.

For the next forty-five minutes, Trevor enjoyed the little ones. They weren't shy with him but told him sincerely what they wanted. Only a couple hung back and he coaxed them forward with jokes and smiles.

Then he looked over to see Mary watching him, her expression full of mirth and interest. He winked at her, looking forward to spending time alone with her. Possibly dinner together. Surely he had earned that.

The last child finished by giving him a big hug, which he returned. He stood and gave a big "ho, ho, ho."

A little boy near him said, "But Santa. You didn't pull out the mistletoe and give Miss Grace a kiss."

As the children erupted in cheers, Grace stood near him to whisper, "Sorry about that. It's sorta tradition here in Charity."

"Well, can't disappoint the paying customers. Where's the mistletoe?"

Grace tried to smile. "In your pocket."

Trevor pulled out the sprig and lifting it over Grace's head, gave her a chaste kiss on the cheek. The children howled with laughter.

He noticed that Grace gave him a small smile as her eyes filled and she hurried from the room.

The teachers and chaperones herded the group out of the restaurant accompanied by a chorus of "thank you's."

Just as Trevor was taking a breath, he saw Joy, Mary, and the other waitresses, quickly cleaning up and preparing for the next group. He looked out the window and saw them coming.

And sighed deeply before he was hurried back to the office.

It was three-thirty and everyone at Hal's Place was exhausted. Joy, Mary, and Trevor were sitting, relaxing in the office. Grace had left when the last group had finished, citing a headache. Mary knew better.

"Well, that was . . . fun." Trevor looked comical, his legs up on another chair, his hands resting on his fat belly, his beard slightly skewed.

Joy sighed deeply and said, "*Sacre bleu*. It is always a 'madhouse' on these days."

Mary chuckled at her expression. "But the kids love it. That's the important thing."

"Yes," Joy said. "I just wish that Mac could have gotten here on time." She cleared her throat and turning to Trevor, added, "Not that you didn't do a wonderful job. It's just that . . . Grace had expected Mac."

"I understand."

Mary's attention went to the fatigued, padded man next to her. "You know, you were pretty good at the Santa thing. Have you done this before?"

She noticed him squirm slightly. "No. Well, maybe. Kind of." His eyes went back and forth between Mary and Joy and tried to explain. "I have a big family. I'm the oldest of seven. I'm familiar with dealing with kids at Christmas."

"That is *magnifique*! We have another day of school children coming tomorrow," Joy said.

Mary grinned at the surprised expression on Trevor's face.

"Oh, I'm sure that Mac will be back by then." He glanced at Mary. "Right?" She laughed aloud as the bell over the front door sounded.

Mac came running into the office, his duffel bag in his hand. "I missed it! I can't believe I missed it!" He dropped his duffel and sighed wearily. "We were on the tarmac ready for take-off when some warning light came on in the cockpit. We had to turn around and wait for another plane."

"Oh, Mac. How very fortunate that you were not in the air when the warning came," Joy said.

He ran his hand over his face in exhaustion. "I guess." Sighing heavily, he said, "How mad is she?"

After a moment of silence as no one knew quite what to say, Mary piped up. "I don't think she's mad. Just disappointed."

Mac grabbed his duffel. "Where is she? Home?" Before the others answered he was heading to the door.

"I suppose this means you're Santa for tomorrow?" Trevor asked hopefully.

Mac grinned at the man. "Yeah, you're off the hook. And thanks for filling in for me. I owe you a dinner." And then he was gone.

"I will add my thanks, Trevor," Joy said. "You, ah, saved the day." She smiled and left.

Leaving Trevor and Mary alone in the quiet office. They looked at each other and shared a smile.

"I must say, you filled the role of Santa well," Mary said. "I guess you could make a few extra dollars during the season, if you wanted." They chuckled.

"It was nothing. And hey, I got two free dinners out of it." Mary chuckled. He moved closer to her and said, "But what I'd really like is if maybe you'd join me. For dinner. Tonight."

Mary couldn't stop the pleasure from showing on her face. "Oh. Well, I guess I could do dinner."

"Great." He really did have an appealing smile. He looked down at his suit and said, "Now, if you wouldn't mind helping me out of my costume, I'd appreciate it."

Mary stood and reached out a hand to pull Trevor, large belly and all, up from his chair. She laughed at his groan. She was finding herself laughing more and more around him. Who would have thought?

They met at a lovely, intimate restaurant in the heart of Charity. The candlelight along with the small lights throughout the restaurant added to the romantic ambiance. The soft Christmas music created a dreamy setting.

Trevor struggled not to stare at the beautiful woman in front of him. Her golden blonde hair glimmered in the dim light. Her eyes shimmered with contentment and fun. And her smile warmed the deep places of his heart that he hadn't realized were cold.

Their conversation flowed, each sharing about his or her life. When she began asking questions about his family, he was careful about his answers. "I have two brothers and four sisters. We all take turns working in my father's grocery store, along with Mom."

"Your father must be grateful for all the help."

Trevor hesitated. "Yes. Although he'd probably tell you that sometimes he could get all the work done faster by himself."

Mary chuckled. "And how did you get into the events planning business?"

He'd tone down his explanation due to his self-consciousness. "I was working at a restaurant and taking courses at N.Y.U. when a friend told me about a position with your mother's company." He wouldn't explain that the "friend" was his boss at the school's cafeteria. And the position was being an errand boy. No reason for Mary to know the details.

"Well, I'm sure she was very glad you came along. She seems to rely on you for everything."

The slight edge to Mary's voice had Trevor stiffening. "I thought we'd resolved that issue. Merrilyn and I are only business associates, you do know that, don't you?"

"Yes, of course." Mary's hand went to cover Trevor's. "I'm . . . well, I'm just sorry that she doesn't feel she can rely on my dad." She sighed quietly and added, "Before she left, she relied on him for everything."

Trevor couldn't help it. Her hand on his felt so good that he turned his over and linked their fingers together. Rubbing his thumb over the back of her hand, he said, "You know there's nothing you can do about that."

She dropped her hands on her lap. "Maybe."

They enjoyed a first course of salad and then steaks for the entrée. Mary conveyed her conversation with Big Jed about the senior citizen group pulling the sleigh. They laughed over Grace's "Hal's Place Float Float." They talked about the children he'd held on his lap that day. It was a relaxing evening, Trevor thought, as they had after-dinner coffees. Perhaps it was a good time to make sure the issue of the events company future was put to rest.

"What did Merrilyn say when you told her you weren't going to be taking her place?"

Mary huffed out a laugh. "No one can take the place of Merrilyn Kennedy Swenson."

"True. But still, she seemed set that you take over the mantle of president."

"Mmm." Mary took a sip of coffee, leaving Trevor to contemplate just what "Mmm" meant.

A few acquaintances of Mary's approached the table to tell her how much they were looking forward to the parade. She smiled politely, as did Trevor, although he really wanted to get back to their previous conversation. He realized the moment had passed and decided to let it go.

After leaving the restaurant, Trevor suggested a walk. They leisurely strolled through town and then to the path that surrounded the downtown lake. Trevor took her hand, enjoying the night sounds of Charity—the soft Christmas music, the laughter of children awaiting the "snow," the greetings of friends meeting for an evening together. Trevor watched this with curiosity. Was it that much different from New York, except on a much smaller scale?

"What are you thinking?"

Mary's question brought him back to the moment and he laughed at himself. Here he was walking in the moonlight with a beautiful woman and he was philosophizing about small town U.S.A.?

He squeezed her hand and said, "Just enjoying the ambiance." Giving her a grin, he added, "And the company."

"I'm glad. When we get to the other side of the lake you get a stunning view of Charity. Especially this time of year with the town lit up for Christmas, it's incredible."

They stopped directly across from the town. He could see Hal's Place, the main street, the tall Christmas tree at the end of the street. Mary looked at her watch and said, "Hey, we're right on time." When Trevor lifted an eyebrow in question, she said, "Just wait for it."

Music sounded from the main street and suddenly the "snowflakes" started to fall. Trevor could hear the cheering across the lake. It was a different perspective of the town. Charming.

They stood looking for a long time. Finally, Trevor leaned closer to Mary, his arm slipping around her middle. "It's nice," he murmured.

"Yeah. Very nice."

Caught up in the moment, Trevor pulled her tighter to himself. He dropped a kiss on her hair. He was rewarded when she leaned her head against his chest. He wondered if she could feel his heart beating wildly. Gently, he turned her in his arms and wrapped her in his embrace. His eyes held hers as that undeniable attraction between them sizzled. Her eyes softened, holding the glow from the lights of the town. Trevor felt he could crawl into them and live on the warmth.

Carefully, as with a precious possession, he gathered her close, bringing his lips to hers. They kissed in the twilight, as everything around them, sights, sounds, smells, all disappeared from the world. Leaving only the two of them.

Trevor kissed her softly, then firmly, his lips moving over hers until she sighed and opened to him, melting against him. He took the kiss deeper, his hands roaming over her back. She tasted of the sweet wine from dinner and smelled of cinnamon cookies. The same cookies served to the children at Hal's Place that day, a sweet memory that would stay with him.

He was lost in the kiss when she put her hand on his chest and broke away. After taking a breath, she said, "That was . . . nice."

He wasn't sure what to think about that glowing assessment. He put his arm around her and looked again at the little town. He kissed her head and said, "Yeah. Very nice."

Mary sighed and leaned against him. They were quiet for a long while.

"Trevor. I've been thinking."

"Yeah?"

"Yes. This whole business with my parents. I think I know of a way to resolve it."

Trevor frowned. "I don't know that you can resolve it. I think it's something they have to work out between themselves."

"Sure, they do. But I can at least give them the opportunity to do that."

"And how will you do that?"

Mary took a deep breath. "I've decided to take my mother up on her offer. I'm going to take over her company."

Chapter Eleven

Trevor froze. His mouth tried to work, but nothing came out. His throat was thick, unable to swallow. He couldn't believe what he'd just heard. His arm dropped from her side and he stood staring into the night.

"It wasn't my intention, but I think if I take over, my mom will have more time to work things out with my dad. There won't be anything keeping her in New York. She could move back to Charity permanently."

"I see," he mumbled. His vision blurred as he saw his dream of running the company, as well as helping his family, drift away like a falling soap bubble in town. What was he going to do?

He glanced at the hopeful eyes of the woman next to him. Maybe he could talk her out of it. "You're making a lot of assumptions about your mother. Perhaps she doesn't want to move from New York."

"Or maybe she just needs a reason to. If she didn't have the obligations in New York, why wouldn't she want to come back to her friends here in Charity?"

"That's supposing that the reasons for her move in the first place aren't still here." He watched as she thought about this.

"Don't worry about that. I'm forming a brilliant plan for getting my parents back together. It can't miss."

He stopped, trying to digest that bit of news. She was ruining everything by this crazy idea that she could fix her parents' marriage. "You actually think you can interfere in lives and get them to do your bidding?" He didn't include his view that she was being selfish, wanting what might not be best for her parents.

"They still love each other, I'm sure of that," she said defensively.

"And you think taking over your mother's job will help them see that?" He shook his head and added, "I just don't see the connection."

He knew he should have stopped there but a question was burning in his mind. "And are you sure you're actually up to running a major New York event planning company?"

One dark eyebrow raised. Yep, he'd probably said the wrong thing.

"Excuse me, but I currently run a successful business and I'm very good at it."

"Of course you are. But . . . well, New York's a bigger pond. The events planning industry is different from real estate."

"Yes, I know. But I'm good with people. I've planned major events before. I'm sure with Mom's advice and her contacts I could slip right into the business."

"What about us?" Okay, that slipped out, but now that he'd said it, he'd continue. "I'd like to get to know you better, spend some time with you." He shook his head. "I can't see that happening if you're . . . my boss."

Mary took a few steps away and rubbed her arms. "You'd . . . like to know me better? Really?"

Trevor cocked his head in confusion. Suddenly, the beautiful and confident woman was gone. In her place was an unsure, nervous girl, shifting on her feet, biting her lower lip. It would have been fascinating if Trevor hadn't been so surprised. In answer to her question, he said, "Yes."

Without looking at him, she said, "That's nice. Really nice. But I'm not really in a place to . . . you know, think about a relationship. Things are really up in the air in my life, with my parents. It's really not a good time."

"Really?" he asked, mocking her overuse of the word.

Her stance became defensive as she stood tall. "Yes. It's not a good time for me to start something." She rubbed her arms harder and said, "I'm getting cold. Let's start back."

He let her walk, all the while studying her. Interesting. "Is that why you only have meaningless relationships? Like with Brad? You're scared?"

That stopped Mary in her tracks. She turned back to him and in a quiet yet firm voice said, "I'm sorry if your ego is hurt. It wasn't my intention." Then before he could comment, she added, "I'll see myself back to my car. Good night."

He watched her go, not attempting to stop her. Apparently he'd hit a hot button.

His hands in his pockets, he walked back to town, his mind working. He had to find out what was going on in that interesting brain of hers. Or else he'd be out of a job and his family would be out of luck.

And Mary Swenson would be out of his life.

"I think the Santa sleigh should be pulled by the varsity football team wearing those cute antler headbands," the perky cheerleader said to Mary as she twisted a big red bow.

"Oh, well, that's an interesting idea. Haley, how about you go grab another spool of the red ribbon?"

A big Christmas tradition in Charity was the making and delivering of Christmas baskets. For several days, the residents of the community would drop by the Presbyterian church in the downtown area to volunteer putting baskets together and/or delivering them to the less fortunate.

Mary listened to the chatter around her as her hands worked on tying ribbons for the baskets. She was thankful for mindless activity. Her own mind was still trying to process what had happened between her and Trevor the night before.

She looked around wondering when her mother would show up. Mary had timed it all out. Her mother would come and then ten minutes later, her father. She'd make sure that they were working at the same table and then since her dad would have his car there, the two of them could deliver baskets together. No problem.

Mary glanced around and saw Grace. There was a sadness in her eyes that tore at Mary's heart. She gave a small wave and Grace returned it. Soon she'd have to sit with her friend and make sure she was okay.

Mary looked one more time at her watch and then pulled out her cell. There was loud chatter around the front door and she turned to see her mother enter, greeting the women that had at one time been her closest friends. Mary couldn't help choke back a few tears watching the women hug. *Why, Mom? Why leave in the first place?*

She motioned for her mother to join her, which she did. Merrilyn was filled with cheer, eager to share news with her daughter.

"I just got the paperwork back from the cable television company for their float. And the garden club and high school band have promised theirs before the day is over."

"Wow, Mom," Mary said, tying off the end of another bow. "You've been busy. I haven't been as successful."

"You will, darling. Trevor wants to go canvassing on Monday with you. He's one of the best. He'll show you all the tricks of the trade for getting volunteers."

Mary swallowed hard. "Can't wait."

Her stomach tightened when she saw the man of interest enter the building. "What's he doing here?" The comment came out before she could stop it.

Merrilyn turned and looked. "Oh, Trevor, over here," she said, motioning him over. "I told him about the event. He wanted to help out."

Mary sighed as Trevor approached. They smiled politely at each other and Mary gave him instructions on putting baskets together and bringing them back so they could add ribbons and wrapping.

Then Mary saw her dad and motioned him over. Merrilyn and Frank nodded at each other, not nearly as polite as Mary and Trevor had been. Before she missed her chance, Mary grabbed her father and pulled him, straightening his sports jacket, to stand next to his mother. "Did you see the new vitamins I put on the breakfast table, Dad? They should be better for your stomach. Oh, and your dental appointment is scheduled for this Friday at nine.

"Now, you wrap the filled basket in the cellophane and Mom, you attach a big red bow. When we get about fifteen, you two can deliver them. Doesn't that sound like fun?"

Her parents looked at her as if she were nuts, but got busy doing what she'd instructed. Mary stood nearby, hoping to hear their conversation. Wanting to hear them at least speak to each other. She went back to forming large red bows to be used and scanning the area, making sure that no one bothered her parents.

Trevor approached, agitation written all over him. He put two filled baskets on the table in front of them and before he could say anything, Mary pulled him away, in order for her parents to work together without distractions. "Thanks. Doing good. I think there are extra baskets out back, if you'd like to bring them in."

His hands on his hips, he said, "There's plenty in here." He glanced at her quiet parents and said with a touch of sarcasm, "How's it going? They talking yet?"

"Shh." She pulled him further away from Merrilyn and Frank. "Keep it down, will you?" she whispered. "They'll hear you."

"Of course, great relationship healer that you are. Silly of me to interfere. And by the way, I think I saw Brad at another table organizing basket contents. Maybe you'd like to go hang out with him. I'm mean, he's safe, isn't he?"

Offended, she said, "Maybe I will. Brad is a very nice man."

"Yeah, I bet. Nice, safe, comfortable. Like a pair of old shoes." He leaned in closer and whispered in her ear, "But I bet he doesn't make you breathless when he kisses you. I bet you don't melt in his arms the way you do mine. I bet your heart doesn't race when he does this." Trevor covertly nibbled the back of her ear, causing her to shudder.

She sighed. "Stop it. I don't—"

"Oh, really?" The raised voice of her mother boomed through the building. "Well, I'm sure if I'm not working fast enough for you, there are other tables that would be happy to have you."

"Not a bad idea. I might actually enjoy working at another table," Frank replied.

"Hey, you got your wish. They're talking," Trevor said with a smirk.

She made a face at him and hurried over to her parents. "Now what's the trouble? You two seemed to be getting along so well."

"Sure we were getting along. We weren't talking. All she had to do was keep her mouth shut."

"All I said was you needed a little more wrap around the edges. Any one could see that."

"Yeah. Everyone could see that nothing's ever good enough for you. You think the people getting these baskets are going to complain? 'Look, Ma, there's not enough wrap around the edge of our basket. Maybe we should take it back.'"

"If a gift basket is worth doing, it's worth doing well. In New York we put together hundreds of—"

"Ah, Mom." Mary gently put her arm around her mother. "That's all right. Listen, you've almost got fifteen done. Why don't you two grab a list from Ben at the door and deliver them?"

"Honey, I've got a meeting in half an hour," Frank said.

"I'm sure your father doesn't want to be trapped in a car with me," Merrilyn added.

Mary thought quickly. "But hey, you two. It's all about giving out these baskets to the less fortunate. Isn't that what's most important?"

"If the homes are nearby, I can take Merrilyn in the NEV," Trevor said.

"Great. Works for me. Think I'll go say 'hi' to Ben." Frank hurried away.

"Thank you, Trevor. You are indeed a gentleman. Just let me freshen up and we can head out." Merrilyn left for the restroom.

Hands on her hips, eyes narrowed, Mary was seething. She was too angry to speak but continued to stare at him.

"Oh, did I louse up your little plan? I was actually trying to help. I mean after all. It's all about the less fortunate getting the baskets. Right?" He walked away a smug grin on his face.

One she would have loved to wipe off.

As much as she tried, Grace couldn't get past her depression over Mac's work. Even with Christmas swirling around her, she shuffled through Hal's, wondering when Mac would be leaving again.

What she needed was a quiet morning alone with her accounting books. Grace had majored in accounting in college and had always loved the logic and stability of adding columns and reconciling spreadsheets. In fact, she'd dreamed of being a C.P.A. in New York, until she'd inherited Hal's Place. And fell in love with Mac.

With the morning rush over, she settled at her desk with a hot cup of coffee to work. It didn't take long to get in the flow of things, the tidy row of numbers, the adding and subtracting.

There was a soft knock at the door. Then the creak of the door opening, but she didn't look up. From the corner of her eye, she saw a napkin set down, a chocolate chip cookie on top. Her favorite. She smiled and reached for it, finally looking up and meeting Mac's eyes. "Thanks."

He didn't speak but pulled up a folding chair to sit next to her.

After her second bite, she took a sip of coffee and said, "Did you want something?"

"Yeah. I want my happy wife back."

She set the cookie down and sighed. "I'm sorry, honey. I just . . ." Her eyes watered. "I guess I want my husband back."

"Grace." He took her hand and held it between his. "You have me. Completely. Don't you know that?"

"Do I? Mac, I know your career is important to you. I respect that. But things are moving so fast, and I feel that I'm . . . losing you." She held up a hand before he could respond. "I know I may be exaggerating, but I married you because I love you and want to be with you. How can I do that when you're on business trips and book tours?"

"I hear you. Really. And I'm considering that as part of every decision I make, I promise. Sweetheart, our marriage is my priority. I'm not going to do anything to hurt that." He rubbed her hand gently.

A tear escaped despite her efforts to hold it back. "What if the book deal goes through and you have to go on an extended tour? How could that not hurt our marriage?"

"There are other options. You could fly out to meet me. I could fly in."

"For a day or two, here and there." She was getting sadder by the moment.

He didn't speak for a moment and she swallowed hard the emotion that wanted to gush out.

"It may not even come to that. The book deal isn't a done deal. Cramer said the publishers are hesitant. You may be worrying about something that might not even happen."

She hated to hear the disappointment behind his words. What did it say about her that a part of her hoped the deal did fall through? She shook her head. "If I know your agent, he'll work it out."

"Maybe. Maybe not." He put an arm around her and pulled her close. Automatically she rested her head on his shoulder. "In the meantime, let's put it away and enjoy Christmas together."

"I want to."

"Then let's." He kissed her head. "How about we go Christmas shopping?"

She sat up. "Now? In the middle of the morning?"

He shrugged. "Why not? You've got competent people working for you. They can handle the place until Pauline comes in later."

The idea made her smile, made her extremely happy. A day with her husband. Why not? "You're sure you can take the time?"

He kissed her hand and looked intensely into her eyes. "To spend with my girl? Of course." Leaning over, his lips met hers, reminding Grace of the love they shared, the commitment they'd made to each other. The threats of work and travel shouldn't come between that.

On a dreamy sigh, she reached her arms around his neck, playing with the edges of his jet-black hair that she loved so much. "All right, Mr. McCrae. Whisk me away."

"It will be my pleasure, Mrs. McCrae."

Mary tried to stay busy after the debacle at the church. Her attitude wasn't the best early the next week when Trevor stopped by her real estate office to take her canvassing for other parade participants. She was just finishing up with a client on the phone when Trevor walked in, dressed in a navy suit, his hair styled, a tight smile on his face. "Ready?" he asked.

He looked too good. Why did he have to look good to her no matter what the situation? There really must be something wrong with her; maybe she needed vitamins.

"Let me put away these files and I'll be ready."

"You sure you want to give up all this for a high pressure job in the city?"

She turned to see him studying her office. Obviously, he wasn't impressed. Defensively, she said, "It may not look like much but it's mine. It pays my bills."

"Hmm. I thought 'Daddy' did that for you."

The stinging comment had her slamming her file drawer shut. "I beg your pardon?"

"I mean you live over his garage. He develops property, you sell property. You two are pretty close. In fact, you seem to be the one making sure he's taken care of—checking his diet, choosing his clothes, making his appointments. Nice little arrangement. I'm surprised you'd be tempted to leave it."

Mary was shocked silent. She faced away from Trevor thinking about what he said. Was that true? Was she her father's keeper?

"Hey, maybe you and Brad should pursue a relationship. Then you could marry and take care of his mother and your father. It could be quite cozy."

She tried to shake off the hurt at his observations of her life. "You're wrong. In everything you've just said." She grabbed her purse, parade flyers, and sign-up clipboard. "But since I only have to put up with you for another few weeks, I'll simply ignore your comments."

He helped her on with her coat and said, "Unless you take over your mother's business. Then you'll be my boss." Until he resigned, which would happen immediately.

"Something to think about. Shall we go?" She didn't wait for his answer but hurried out of the office.

They started in the same building that housed her office, speaking with each organization. Trevor was amazed at Mary's knowledge of names. She seemed to know everyone.

And everyone knew her, and liked her. The water company joked with her about their ad on her giveaway calendars. A fitness company thanked her for helping to sponsor their recent charity run and promised bottled water for parade participants. The Spanish restaurant offered to let her have a taste of a new chicken dish they were introducing. With everyone she was friendly, authentic, likeable.

Trevor scowled. She really would do well in the event planning business.

As they walked down the street, two familiar faces came toward them. It was Joy and her little girl, holding hands. Trevor racked his brain for the name. It was a flower. Rose? Lily? No, it reminded him of Christmas. Holly, that was it.

"Good morning, Mary. Trevor. How are you today?" Joy asked in her lilted accent.

"Great. Just trying to get more volunteers for the parade."

"Oh, Mary! I just can't wait," Holly said, giving a little bounce. "I'm going to be twirling my baton down Main Street. And I'm going to wear my red sparkling outfit with the green beads. *Belle-mere* made it for me!"

"And I'm sure you'll be gorgeous in it, honey," Mary said kissing Holly's cheek.

"Trevor, I am so happy that you are helping Mary. The town put a heavy responsibility on her." Joy smiled warmly.

"I'm sure she could have handled it, but it's been interesting getting to know your town."

"It is a wonderful place. I am so happy that it is my home now. And the home of my family." Joy squeezed Holly's hand as the little girl beamed at her. Trevor watched the interaction, curious as to their story.

"We are off to buy presents now," Joy said. "Trevor, it was good to see you. Mary, we will have lunch soon and you can tell me about the parade."

Joy angled away from Trevor but he could still see her wiggle her eyebrows at Mary. He fought the urge to explain to Joy that Mary wasn't interested in any kind of relationship with him. She was too busy trying to save her parents' doomed marriage.

Instead, he said, "Nice to see you, Joy. And you Holly. I'm looking forward to your twirling baton come Christmas Eve." She giggled making him smile.

"Mary, you're still taking me ice skating tomorrow night, right?"

"Of course I am, little angel. Wouldn't miss it." Mary gave Holly another kiss on the cheek before she and her stepmother walked off.

"Cute kid," Trevor said as they started down the road.

"Yes she is. A very sweet little girl."

"You're related, right?"

Mary looked up at him, surprised that he'd remembered that detail. "Yes. Her father, Ross, is my cousin." Her attention was straight ahead as if remembering. "My father was developing properties all over Central Florida. We found Charity and moved here years ago. When Ross's wife, Sarah, was diagnosed with terminal cancer, she started looking for a small town for her family. She wanted them to have a place that would love them and care for them when she passed. I recommended Charity, helped them buy their house." Mary sighed deeply. "They weren't here very long before she passed away."

"That's rough. Especially on the kids."

"Yeah. But Sarah was right. Charity has taken care of them. And then last year Ross and Joy fell in love. It was just what the family needed."

"Hmm." Trevor thought about his own family. What would they do if his father didn't recover? He'd keep the idea of Charity in the back of his mind.

They turned the corner and walked to a toy store. It made him think of Holly. "So, you're taking Holly ice skating? Where?"

"Right here. You saw the little rink."

"The 'plastic ice' rink? Are you kidding me?"

"You have no sense of adventure," she teased. "It's fun. Different." Her eyes gleamed with mischief. "Maybe you'd like to join us. Unless you're not that great of a skater."

He snorted. "You think I'd let a Floridian show me, a New Yorker, up on ice skates? You're on."

"Good."

The owners of the toyshop were excited with the ideas that Mary had for their float—Santa's toy workshop. Trevor watched as Mary's eyes lit up explaining how easy it would be to put their float together. And how adorable, and how it would promote the beloved shop.

She really was amazing. Every time he thought he had her pegged, she revealed bits about herself that intrigued him. Today he was seeing a warm, kind layer that he hadn't seen before. He saw a confidence, a talent that caused a beauty to rise up from within.

The fact that she'd not pushed off the parade on others spoke volumes of her love for the town. Of her work ethic, her integrity. Perhaps she could make a go of the Kennedy Swenson company in New York.

A question that the shop owner asked caught his attention. Was Mary having a float in the parade for her real estate business? She laughed it off saying that she hadn't any time. With the event coming up, he knew she must be having to neglect her own business.

Trevor's mind was whirling. There may not be a hope of a relationship for them but he wanted to do something for Mary. Something nice. He excused himself and went outside to make a call.

And set the ball in motion.

Chapter Twelve

"Where's Elena?" Mary asked as she and her mom sat in the dining room for dinner.

"I gave her the night off. She, ah, has a date." Merrilyn smiled as she put a helping of chicken tetrazzini on her daughter's plate.

Mary was delighted. It had been one of her favorite meals, back in the day when her mother ran their kitchen. Her mind came back to her mother's words and she chuckled. "Big Jed?"

"Mmm. That's what I surmise. She was very excited. I'm hoping to catch her when she comes in and get all the details." The two women giggled like teenagers over the idea.

The laughter stopped when Frank walked into the room. He'd stopped taking his meals at home, another concern for Mary. "Hey, Dad. It's chicken tetrazzini. You want some?"

Frank glanced at Merrilyn and then his daughter. "It . . . smells good. I suppose I could go for a bite."

"I'll get you a plate and utensils." Merrilyn jumped up and hurried to the kitchen. Mary sighed in relief. Hopefully the tiff they'd had when making

Christmas baskets was over. Maybe things could move forward now.

In a whisper, Frank said, "You make this, Mary?"

"Nope. Mom did. Remember how good it used to be?" She looked hopefully at her father.

Merrilyn returned and placed a plate, utensils, napkin, and glass of tea in front of Frank, who was sitting next to Mary. She returned to her seat and the three quietly ate dinner.

Mary watched them, looking for any opening that would allow her to ease things between them. Then decided that perhaps the silence was good enough for the moment.

"Do you have plans with your young man tonight, dear?" Merrilyn asked.

"What? Ah, what young man do you mean mother?" Mary hadn't even thought of Brad since Trevor had first kissed her.

"Why, Brad, of course." She lifted an eyebrow. "Is there another young man that I don't know about?"

"No! No, no. But really Brad isn't my young man. We . . . just go out occasionally."

Merrilyn set her fork down and studying her daughter, said, "That concerns me, Mary. You're a beautiful, interesting woman. You should have your pick of beaus to spend time with. Instead you're wasting away living in a small town where your options are slim."

Mary did not want to go in that direction. She could see her father's expression harden slightly. "Charity is a wonderful town, mother. In fact, you used to love living here." A sad look came to her mother's eyes and Mary quickly added, "Did you see Hannah Simcox's new hairdo? I heard her husband thinks it's her evil twin."

Merrilyn chuckled just as Mary had hoped. If anything could cheer up her mother it would be gossip from around the town.

"I'll have to find out what salon she uses. And stay far from it."

"You never did answer your mother about your plans for tonight," Frank said, his eyes on his food as he continued to eat.

"Oh, yes. I'm taking Holly ice skating downtown."

"What a sweet little girl. That sounds like fun."

And there was her opening. "Yes. How about you two come with me? Mom, you could check out Hannah's hair. She runs the ticket booth. Dad, the bakery has that gingerbread you like. And you could both try out the ice skating rink. How about it?"" Her brows raised high, she waited.

"I don't know, Mary. I have some work to go over tonight," Frank said.

"Oh, come on, Dad. We haven't had some fun together in a while now."

"Maybe your mother has something else planned."

"Your father doesn't want to go, honey. Besides, he probably doesn't even remember how to ice skate. He doesn't want to make a fool of himself."

"Who says I'll make a fool of myself?"

"Of course you won't. Please, Dad. Mom." Mary added the wide eyes, the hopeful grin that she knew could melt her parents. There were benefits to being the only child.

Merrilyn looked at Frank. "Well?"

He shrugged. "All right, I'll go. I do like that gingerbread."

They went back to eating, Mary smiling smugly. It was quiet for a few minutes. Then Frank muttered, "The chicken's good, Merry."

"Thank you, Frank," she said, not looking at him.

It wasn't the UN Peace talks but it was progress.

They went early to the small skating rink set up on the main street of Charity, hoping to beat the crowd. They'd stopped to pick up Holly and the little girl clasped Mary's hand, her body bouncing with energy and excitement.

The foursome rented skates and started on the plastic rink. Holly whooped and squealed, trying to keep her balance. She saw a couple of her friends and skated ahead. Mary smiled warmly at her cousin, envying her simple joy of the season. She so wanted to enjoy Christmas with both her parents for a change.

"You sure you don't need a walker to help you along?"

Mary turned to see Trevor skating beside her. She glanced at the walkers that were there for the new skaters to prevent nasty falls. She snorted and said, "I do just fine, thank you." She continued skating, trying to distance herself from the man.

But he wouldn't let her. "I can't believe a Florida girl can ice skate." There was that haughty grin again. "Know any tricks?"

"Yes. But I won't do them here. And I suggest you refrain as well. This rink isn't built for that."

Trevor looked down at the surface that his skates were gliding over. "I suppose."

After a moment, Trevor cleared his throat. "I . . . apologize for coming down so hard on you. It's really none of my business what your relationship with your father is. I shouldn't have interfered."

Mary was surprised and gladdened at his apology. Wanting to put their differences behind them, she smiled and said, "There's a large skating rink about ten miles down the road outside of Kissimmee. That's were you should go for real ice skating. Maybe I could show you sometime." Mary continued to watch Holly.

She felt Trevor's hand taking her arm and wrapping it around his. She turned and was captured by his eyes, a dazzling green that seemed to shine at her.

They settled into a comfortable pace, her mother and father skating in front of them. Christmas music softly played. Happiness filled her heart. Perhaps Christmas was the time for miracles. She and her family could sure use one.

She glanced next to her at the handsome man that skated alongside. And desired to spend more time with him, to fully restore the peace between them.

"I'm making cookies Saturday. I sure could use some help." She turned her wide smile at him. "Care to join me?"

He hesitated and then said, "If samples are included in the job."

Yes, this Christmas kept getting better and better.

Her happiness lasted for less than five minutes.

Mary and Trevor continued to skate together, chatting amicably. The snow had started on Main Street, bringing more people. As the noise level increased, along with the number of skaters, Mary lost track of her parents. She stopped to look around, nearly getting bumped by a couple of teenagers.

"Is something wrong?" Trevor asked.

"My parents. I don't see them."

Trevor led Mary to the side of the rink as they searched. And finally found them.

"All I said was you could have used a bit less salt in the chicken." Frank was busy taking off his skates as his wife stood next to him, her hands on her hips scowling.

"Frank Swenson, you know that casserole was perfect. It was like I always made it. I didn't change anything."

"Well maybe my tastes have changed," he snapped, grabbing his skates and heading for the exit.

"Don't you walk away from me. I haven't finished talking to you!" Merrilyn hobbled over to the exit in her skates, yelling the entire time.

Frank ignored her, turned in his skates, and headed to the nearby bakery.

"That man," Merrilyn muttered, shaking with rage.

"Ma'am. I need those skates back if you're finished skating."

"Hm?" Merrilyn saw a teenage boy at the exit waiting. "Oh, of course." She sat at a bench and quickly removed the skates. As Mary approached, she called to her. "Sweetheart, I'm walking home. Trevor. I didn't see you. Did you need something?"

Trevor stuck his hands in his pockets looking guilty. "No, Merrilyn. Just thought I'd soak up a little atmosphere."

"I see. Well, I need you first thing in the morning. I'd like to contact Benjamin Crandall and work out a few details for his event."

"I'll be there by eight."

Mary watched her mother huff off into the night. She sighed deeply, again feeling the weight of her divided family. She sat and began unlacing her skates.

Trevor joined her and gently put his hand over hers. "I'm sorry, Mary."

How could he understand what she was going through? His large, happy family was probably enjoying the season right now as she sat there depressed. But it wasn't his fault, she had to remember that.

She gave him a tentative smile. "I enjoyed the skating, Trevor. I think I'll go sit with my father now until Holly's done skating." She stood and said, "I'll see you Saturday?"

Saturday afternoon, Mary had everything ready to make Christmas cookies. The flour, sugar, butter, milk, eggs, cookie cutters, and various toppings were all lined up on the counter of her parents' kitchen. Since her kitchen was so small, she always used the gourmet kitchen to make her special cookies.

But this year she had a helper. A smile instantly came to her face thinking of Trevor. The more time she spent with the man, the more she liked him. Not entirely wise, she knew, but with all the stress of this season—the parade, her parents—she felt she deserved a little enjoyment. And Trevor would fit the bill.

The doorbell rang and she ran to answer it. There he stood in jeans and a New York Yankees tee shirt. His hair was gently mussed from the wind and the sunglasses he wore gave him a slightly mysterious look. Very sexy.

With a smile on her face, she said, "Hey."

"Hi." Grinning, He took his glasses off and hooked them in his front pocket. She enjoyed the head to toe look he gave her, seeing approval in his eyes. "Love the apron," he said casually as he entered the house.

Mary laughed. Her father had given her the bright red apron that said, "From Mrs. Claus's Kitchen."

"Hey, maybe you can be Mrs. Claus, sitting with Big Jed on the float in the parade," he teased.

"I think Elena might have something to say about that," she said with more laughter.

"Maybe I would too," he said in that low voice that caused a delicious hum through her body.

As they stood looking at each other, footsteps sounded on the stairs. "Trevor. What are doing here? It's your day off."

Trevor's gaze flew to her mother. "Oh, I thought I'd help Mary make cookies. I've been promised samples."

Merrilyn studied the pair. "Of course. She used to let her father be a taster. That's very nice of you, Trevor." She walked to a hook behind the door and took her purse. "I'm going out to tea with Harriet Wingate." She gave them one more look. "Remember not to overcook the cookies, dear. It makes them hard."

"I'll remember. Have a nice time." Mary blew out a breath, deciding to put her mother and her father out of her mind for the rest of the day and just enjoy baking. And spending time with Trevor.

He slapped his hands together. "Okay. Tell me what to do."

In the kitchen, Mary washed her hands and said, "You didn't make cookies with your family when you were growing up?"

He hip-bumped her away from the sink so he could wash his hands. "Not really. My mom and sisters did, I guess. I was always helping my father in the store."

Mary gave him instructions about mixing the dry ingredients while she handled the butter and sugar. "It sounds like you worked hard growing up."

He shrugged. "There was always a lot to get done."

"Are your parents upset that you won't be spending Christmas with them this year?"

"The others are there. Along with a few grandchildren to distract them. I told them I'd see them on New Years."

"So, you'll leave after Christmas?"

"Yes. The day after Christmas."

It was silent as she pondered the short amount of time they had to be together. Although, if she took over her mother's company, they'd be together in New York. Something to think about.

Mary smiled and said, "Well, all the more reason for you to taste the best homemade Christmas cookies that you'll ever have."

"I can't wait," he said, giving her a genuine smile.

Chapter Thirteen

They made sugar cookies. They made gingerbread cookies. They made chocolate chip cookies, a favorite of Mary's father. After the dozens and dozens of cookies were removed from the oven, the kitchen looked like a war zone. Mary started a sink of hot, soapy water and Trevor stacked dirty bowls, wiping the large island.

Their conversation had been pleasant, teasing, funny, interesting. Neither spoke of family but about their own lives, interests, and hobbies.

Trevor was again amazed at how intelligent Mary was. She'd graduated in the top five percent of her class at Columbia. She was athletic, enjoying all sports, trying new ones. She had a sharp sense of humor that kept him on his toes. He could really see himself falling for this girl if not for . . .

Where did he begin? Her life was here in Central Florida, a small town. His was in New York. Unless, of course she decided to become his boss, which would completely ruin his plans. His family needed him and was depending on him. Could he continue working for Kennedy Swenson Events with Mary at the helm, hoping for substantial bonuses that would see his family through his father's illness?

But no, he'd keep those thoughts away, at least today. He'd enjoy a charming, beautiful woman who made him laugh.

"And then Holly wanted to know about her twirling group dressing like elves for the parade. I said I thought that they would be adorable as elves, but I had to check . . . What is it?"

"Hmm?"

"You're staring at me."

Trevor lightly shook his head. "Nothing wrong with staring at a beautiful woman." He loved that the comment made Mary blush. "You've got a little something on your face," he said moving closer, grinning. She didn't, but he wanted so much to touch her.

His finger gently caressed her cheek. Then his hand stretched to hold her face as he gazed into the blue depths of her eyes. Holding her head steady, he moved those last few inches and touched his lips to hers. The contact was light, but the intensity wasn't. A jolt shot straight through him as he put his free arm around her waist and pulled her closer. His lips rubbed against hers and when she sighed, he took the opportunity to take the kiss deeper.

He relaxed, holding her tightly to him, feeling a sense of coming home, like he was where he was supposed to be. Her hands slowly went around his waist and up his back and he allowed himself the luxury of taking the sweetness, the contentment, as well as the passion. And forgetting everything else.

Mary was dying. What was he doing to her? After the debacle that was her parents' marriage, she had no desire for a serious relationship of any kind.

So why was she folded around this man as if he were the only port in a raging storm? The answer was simple. And complicated. She was falling in love with him. Big time. He was everything she could have asked for in a man— hard-working, interesting, handsome. The chemistry between them was off the charts. He respected her and at the same time challenged her. It was an addictive combination.

Trevor left her lips to rain little kisses over her cheek, to her ear, hitting that sensitive spot behind the earlobe, making her shiver.

And her mind turned off. She turned his head back and took his lips, her passion threatening to scorch.

"Mary, I'm going to—"

She and Trevor jumped back as if hit by lightning. Her father stood in the doorway, watching them, glaring.

"Ah, yes, Dad?" she said smoothing her hair with her nervous fingers.

"I'm going over to the Lake Nona site for a few hours to check on a couple of things." He looked around. "Where's your mother?"

"Having tea with Harriet Wingate."

"I don't want anyone to expect me for dinner. I'm eating out," he said and then left.

"I'll leave a note," Mary called out just before the front door slammed. "Well, that was embarrassing."

"Your father does know that you kiss men on occasion, doesn't he?"

"I suppose." She turned to him. "I'm pretty sure he was surprised that you were one of them," she teased.

"Lucky me," he said as he indulged himself in one more steamy kiss. He pulled back and grinned. "You wash, I dry."

After an exhausting day of baking, Trevor offered to treat her to dinner at Hal's Place. Especially since Trevor had two free meals coming his way. Pauline seated them in a booth in the back giving Mary a wink, which caused her to mentally shake her head.

"I'm not creating a scandal by having dinner here with you, am I?" he asked.

"No. No," she repeated as she opened her menu. "It's just one of the hazards of small town living." She looked up, giving him a little smile. "I don't mind Trevor. Really."

He took her hand and returned the smile.

"Hey, you two know what you're going to have?" A happy Grace stood before their booth, pad and pen ready.

Mary was glad to see her friend. She'd been worried about Grace since Mac had missed the first day of the Christmas field trips to the diner. "You doing all right, Grace?"

Her authentic smile lightened Mary's heart. "Yeah. I'm fine." She shyly looked down and said, "Mac felt terrible about missing that first day as Santa. But we talked all about it. And made up. Everything's good."

"He's not going to have to continue to travel for work?"

A slight thread of tension weaved through her face. "I didn't say that. But we've decided not to let it ruin our Christmas. The holidays are a time for coming together, remembering what you have, not arguing about the future."

"I think that's wise," Trevor added.

"Yeah. Oh, and Mac's heading the work on the Hal's Place Float . . . ah, Float. It's going to be awesome."

"Glad to hear it."

A small grin edged Grace's lips up. "So, you two out on a . . . *date* tonight?"

Her face heating, Mary sat back, putting her hands in her lap. "Trevor thought he'd redeem his two free meals, so here we are," Mary said, hoping to at least lessen her friend's interest. It was an impossible task.

Trevor didn't help when he said, "We made Christmas cookies all afternoon and needed a night out."

Grace's smile widened. "I'm delighted that you chose to come to Hal's Place for your date. Now what can I get for you?"

Mary felt her face turn beet red as Trevor ordered burgers and fries for them.

"Hey there, pretty Mary. Didn't see you two over here in the corner." As if things couldn't have gotten worse, there stood Big Jed, the town's biggest gossip, standing before them, his arm firmly around Elena.

They looked so cute together that Mary had to grin. "Hey, Big Jed. Elena." Elena's sweet smile warmed her heart. She was glad that the two had found each other.

"How about we join you, make it a double date. Hadn't had one of those in pert near fifty years." Before Mary or Trevor could comment, Jed said, "Now Trevor, you get on Mary's side so we can have the other side." He moved aside so that Trevor could get up, and then grabbing Elena's hand slid into the booth. "Grace, could you get us a couple of number three combos?"

"I hope we are not intruding," Elena said quietly.

Trevor stretched his arm on the bench seat behind Mary. His other hand went to rest gently on her knee. "On the contrary, Elena. So glad you joined us." He squeezed Mary's knee and winked at her.

"I'm really glad to see you Mary," Jed started. "I wanted to talk to you about the parade."

"Sure, Big Jed," Mary said as she thanked Grace for the water and then took a sip.

"I had a great idea for what to get to pull the sleigh in the parade. Since we're celebrating Charity, the parade should show a Florida

Christmas. And what's more Florida than . . ." He hesitated, clearly to build anticipation. "Alligators."

Trevor choked on his water. Mary's jaw dropped, waiting for speech to return.

"It makes all kinds of sense. We can harness a group of trained alligators, maybe from Gatorland down the road, and then have a couple of their handlers guide them down the parade route. Huh?" Clearly proud of himself, Big Jed leaned back in his seat, Elena looking adoringly up at him.

"Uh . . . Big Jed, I'm not sure what to say," Mary muttered.

"Don't it beat all? We'd be the envy of every other Christmas parade, I bet."

Mary and Trevor looked at each other. Trevor cleared his throat and said, "That's a great idea, Big Jed, but unfortunately it has a few problems."

"Yeah? How's that?"

"First of all, if we harness a group of alligators, we'll have every wildlife and animal activists group in the country bringing lawsuits."

"That's good, that's very good," Mary mumbled.

"Second . . . I don't think parents with children would be too keen to see a group of alligators being led down the street. You're liable to scare off your spectators."

"You think so? Why ol' Albert that lives in the lake wouldn't hurt a soul."

"And thirdly, and probably most important. If anything goes wrong, anything at all, the town would never be able to recover—not financially or in reputation. All it would take would be for one alligator to get loose and . . ." Trevor shuddered slightly. "I don't even want to think about it."

Big Jed scratched his chin as he thought. "You bring up a lot of good points. Just thought it'd be a hoot. Maybe you're right."

Mary and Trevor both let out quiet sighs of relief.

"Come on, Elena," he said gently pushing her out. "Let's go see what we can play on the jukebox. Bet there's a real romantic song I can play for you." The woman actually giggled as he took her hand and led her away.

Trevor and Mary were silent for a moment. Then Mary took Trevor's hand and held it tightly. "I owe you. Big Time."

That night after a romantic walk around town, they made their way back to the Swenson home.

Mary invited Trevor in to watch a movie on her father's large screen in the den. *The Grinch* happened to be on so they sat to enjoy Jim Carrey's portrayal of the famous Dr. Seuss character.

Before the back story of the Grinch was fully told, Trevor had his arms around Mary, and they cuddled, watching the movie. Trevor could not remember enjoying a movie more.

But soon, the movie was lost in the background as the scents of vanilla, butter, and sugar hit him and he thought of their day cooking

Christmas treats together. His heart thudded in his chest and he wanted nothing more than to kiss the incredible woman beside him.

After a big sniff, he tenderly kissed her head. Then her ear, her cheek. She moved her head so their lips could meet and the sweetness of their homemade cookies weren't a match for the sweetness of their kiss.

Mary cupped his face in her hands and gently kissed him, as if pouring her heart out to him. The scary thing was, he wanted to take that heart and treasure it. Never letting it go. He returned the kiss, holding her closer, running his hands up and down her back.

Trevor had the irrational compulsion to tell her he was falling in love with her. It would scare her, make her run, for sure. But that's how he felt. "Mary," he whispered between kisses.

Her soft blue eyes looked up at him and he nearly fell at her feet. She was so beautiful, so . . . right for him. He wanted her with a passion he'd never felt before.

Words seemed meaningless at the moment, when all he wanted was to show her how much she meant to him. Gently, he eased her down on the cushions of the couch to get more comfortable, their lips fused. Their bodies seemed to fit together like a perfect puzzle. He wasn't surprised. When she massaged the back of his neck, he shuddered, holding her tightly to him.

They kissed as hands caressed, hearts beat, breaths mingled. In the far corners of his mind, he heard a door open and then slam.

Mary had had one of the most wonderful days of her life and at the moment, kissing Trevor, she didn't want it to end.

As if fate had something different to say about it, she heard the loud voices down the hall.

"I don't care what you serve at the party, Merry. I'm not even sure that I'm coming."

"Oh, yes you are, Frank Swenson. You're going to be here and put on a happy face to greet all our friends if I have to threaten you to within an inch of your life!"

Mary tensed underneath Trevor and he gave her a sad smile.

"I don't want a party, Merry! Haven't I got that through to you? I remember the last party we had and I lost a wife out of that one!"

Mary frowned.

"Why do you think I want another one?"

"Because of your daughter." They heard Frank groan. "I'm serious. She needs to be at parties, she needs to be mingling and entertaining. It's in her blood, it's her destiny."

"Oh, give me a break, will you."

Before they could move to sit up, the door to the den flew open and her father was standing in the doorway, arms crossed, scowling. "You want to tell me what you're doing with my daughter?"

Chapter Fourteen

Mary wondered if you could actually die of embarrassment.

"Frank? Whom are you speaking with?" Her mother arrived just in time to see the two of them sitting up, Trevor straightening his shirt, Mary finger combing her hair. "What . . . Mary? Trevor?" Merrilyn's shocked expression would have been comical if the situation had been different.

"Trevor and I . . . were just watching a movie. See?" she pointed to the television. "The Grinch."

"Seems a little difficult to watch a movie from the position you two were in," Frank murmured.

"Trevor? Mary? I'd like an explanation. Now please?"

She and Trevor stood, exchanging glances. What was she to say?

Trevor cleared his throat. "Ah, Mr. Swenson. Merrilyn."

"At this moment I am Mrs. Swenson, Mary's mother, if you don't mind." Merrilyn folded her arms. Mary noticed Frank's approving look at her mother's comment.

"Okay. Mr. and Mrs. Swenson." He took Mary's hand in his. "I . . . well, I'm seeing your daughter. I hope this doesn't cause problems for either of you. Merr—I mean Mrs. Swenson. You know me, you know that I'm a good guy. Mr. Swenson, I hope that we can at least be civil with each other. Regardless, Mary and I are both adults and I happen to think that our relationship is our business. Right?" he asked turning to Mary.

"Right," she said hesitantly, watching her parents. Hoping for the best.

No one spoke for a long moment. Frank and Merrilyn looked at each other. Then Frank said, "It's your own fault Merry. Bringing some upstart New Yorker here, dangling him in front of our daughter. It would serve you right if she ran off with the boy and you never saw her again," He said storming out of the room.

"My fault? My fault!" Merrilyn followed Frank out, her loud voice echoing through the house. "She lives with you in this small town with no options and you blame me? Of course she falls for the first fascinating man that comes along. She needs passion in her life." Merrilyn followed Frank out.

"Oh, spare me. Passion?" Frank's footsteps sounded on the stairs. "We are not going to have this conversation."

The movie continued to play, neither Mary nor Trevor speaking for a moment.

"Again. I apologize for my parents," she whispered.

He put an arm around her and rubbed her arm. "Don't let them upset you, okay?"

She nodded. "I did learn something new tonight. Dad lost Mom because of a party? I've never heard that before."

"Seems strange that Merrilyn is so determined to have a party here if it brings back bad memories."

"Yes. It does seem strange." She stared straight ahead, her mind spinning. "And you know what? It gives me a direction to go in." She looked at him and said, "Trevor. I know how to get them back together."

Trevor grimaced, dropping his arm. "Mary, I really don't think it's a good idea for you to get involved in their relationship."

"They need my help. They've had five years on their own and look what's happened. Nothing. Dad said he lost his wife because of a party. I think we need to have a phenomenal party, let them see how well they are together, let them see each other at their best. Rekindle some of those good feelings and erase that party that drove them apart. It could work."

"Or, your butting in could cause a deeper division between them, driving them to make their separation permanent."

She frowned and set her hands firmly on her hips. "You're an optimist. Why don't you help me instead of predicting doom and gloom?"

"I'm a realist. And there's no chance that you're going to get me in the middle of your parents marriage."

"Don't you want them to get back together?"

"Honey, I want what's best for them. And you. And us." He took both her hands and smiled.

She squeezed the hands and said, "I hear you, Trevor. But I . . . I don't feel that I can have a serious relationship until this thing with my parents is decided."

"You seemed to be doing okay before they walked in," he said, his voice carrying a little irritation with it.

Annoyed she dropped his hands. "Maybe I shouldn't have been."

Trevor put one arm around her waist. "Okay, okay. You're conflicted because of your parents. I know you love them." He kissed her brow. "I get that, I do. But some time you're going to have to accept their decisions, either way. And make a few of your own. Like if you're going to take over your mother's company."

She saw his eyebrows lift. At that moment it hit her squarely between the eyes that he was concerned about his job. Her heart softened as she realized she'd never considered how this would affect him.

"Oh, Trevor." She gave him a hug and sighed. "I know this concerns your career and that's not fair to you. Just give me until Christmas to see what happens with these two. Then if the question of the company is still up in the air we'll, sit down and talk it out. I don't want you to worry about it."

Sighing, he said, "I guess that will have to do for now." He kissed her briefly. "I'd better get going. Thanks for a great day, Mary. I mean that."

"It was a great day," she said, smiling as she walked him out.

Even though she had no idea what the future held for either of them.

"How's Dad doing today?" Trevor asked as he spoke with his mom.

"He had a bad day yesterday, honey. It was hard for him to breath." Trevor's mother hesitated and then said, "Doctor Bremer said the new treatment would do him wonders. Any word on your bonus?"

Trevor sighed heavily and ran his fingers through his hair in frustration. "No. Things are pretty screwy with the company right now, Mom. Could be having a change in presidents."

"Oh, Trevor. Do you think that you—"

"I wasn't talking about me. Remember that daughter that I told you about?"

"Yeah. Mary. The one that's got your interest?"

Trevor ignored that. "She could very well be the next president of Kennedy Swenson Events. That is, if Merrilyn has anything to say about it."

There was a pause in the conversation before his mother asked, "And where does that put you?"

"I have no earthly idea, Mom. I thought I was coming south with Merrilyn to help her with business. But her relationships with her husband and daughter are so strange, you wouldn't believe it. I wonder if this whole trip wasn't just an excuse for her to see them again."

"I'm confused."

"Join the club."

He could hear his mother sigh. "Be careful, son. You don't want to get in the middle of a family's problems." She hesitated and then said, "Maybe you should just come back to New York. I'm sure you could get on with any event company in the city. Merrilyn would surely give you a great letter of recommendation."

"I've thought about that, but I don't know, Mom. I should just talk to Merrilyn about the bonus. I know that you and Dad were counting on it."

"We'll make do. You have to do what's right for you. Now, let's talk about Mary." Trevor cringed, knowing what was coming next. "How do your feelings for her play into all this?"

"She's . . . she's got me wound up in knots. But she's consumed with her parents, trying to get them to kiss and makeup. I'm afraid that I'm getting in too deep here, just spinning my wheels."

"Then you should think of coming home, son. The sooner, the better."

It was the calm before the storm—the day of the Swenson Christmas party.

The house was peaceful as Mary found her father in the kitchen having a cup of coffee before going in to the office. Merrilyn had gone to have her hair and nails done. The florist was due at noon and the caterer at four so this would be the only quiet time of the day in the Swenson home.

Mary got a cup of coffee and joined her father. "Need some company, Dad?"

"Need some peace and quiet. But your mother's made sure that's not happening."

"Don't be so hard on her. It's been . . . interesting having her here this Christmas, wouldn't you say?"

"Interesting is a kind word for it." He took a sip. "And don't you think of skipping out on this party tonight, missy. If I've got to be here, so have you."

"I wouldn't miss it, Dad." To his amused expression, she added, "Really."

They settled into a comfortable silence, each enjoying their cup of coffee.

Mary decided that the time was right for approaching the subject that had been on her mind since last Saturday night. "So, you and Mom used to have a lot of parties, right?"

"You were here, you know that," he mumbled.

"You used to like them. You used to say that my mother was the best hostess that ever was. You called her 'the hostess with the mostess.'"

"I remember," he said quietly.

Mary was through with being subtle. She put her hand over her father's and said, "What happened Dad? The other night you mentioned losing your wife because of a party. Why? Tell me."

Frank's sad eyes looked up at Mary. The edges of his lips lifted slightly as if he wanted to give her a smile. "I can't tell you much, pumpkin. Because I don't really know."

Mary narrowed her eyes. "What do you mean?"

A sigh of frustration escaped his lips. "Five years ago we had a New Year's Eve party. It was a blowout as usual. Big, loud, elegant, glitzy. The party ended at about two in the morning and when the last guest left, your mother turned on me like I was a monster, yelling at me at the top of her lungs. I didn't get all the words, but I got the jest. I wasn't good enough for her, I was lower than a skunk. I was tired, didn't want to deal with it, so I went to bed.

"The next morning, she was packing. Said she was moving to New York to start her life over. I tried to reason with her, get her to talk to me, but she refused. Said she wasn't going to live with a philanderer. Like I'd ever step out on your mother. I was crazy about her, there was never anyone else for me. I figured she just wanted out of our marriage. What could I do?"

Tears filled Mary's eyes as she listened. It just didn't make sense to her.

"I figured she'd go to New York and either get tired of it and come home or else I'd get divorce papers. When neither happened, I . . . well, I just didn't know what to think. I still don't."

"Dad, why didn't you ask her?"

"I did, countless times. She told me all she was going to. And why should I go crawling back to her, begging her to come home? I've got my pride, don't I?"

Mary sat back in her chair, astounded. "Yes. You've both got your pride. I hope you're happy with it, because it won't keep you warm on a cold night. Or be there for you when you've had a bad day and need someone to lift you up. It won't keep you from getting lonely."

She sat up straight in her chair and said, "Let me ask you just one question. Do you still love Mom?"

Frank looked ahead, not saying anything for so long that Mary thought he wouldn't answer her. He turned his head and said, "Merry Swenson was the love of my life. And for better or worse, nothing's changed that."

Mary's heart lightened. "Then tell her! She needs to know that before she thinks she has to go back to New York."

Frank played with the rim of his coffee cup. "I'll think about what you've said, Mary. But I make no promises."

"I understand." And she did.

She couldn't wait until the party. It was going to be one to remember, she was just sure about it.

Trevor's mind wouldn't rest. His options kept whirling through his head, each with both pros and cons. But the overriding theme of his thoughts was Mary. What was he going to do about her—just go back to New York and forget her?

It was two days before the Christmas Eve parade. The event details had been finalized and everything was in place. The Swenson's big Christmas party was tonight and he had to make an appearance. He desperately wanted to see Mary. Even though it frustrated him to watch her put so much energy and emotion in trying to make her parents reunite. But he was powerless to help.

He sat at Hal's Place with a mug of hot chocolate, working on notes for the events planned in January and February. Hopefully he'd still have a job. He wasn't so sure. No matter what, he'd decided to still approach Merrilyn about his bonus. His father needed treatment for his emphysema.

Several people had stopped by his booth to tell him how excited they were about the parade. Some even showed him a hat they'd be wearing or a dance move they'd be performing. It was an interesting little town.

The bell over the front door jingled and he saw Brad Moore walk into the restaurant. He again studied the man wondering why Mary had dated him to begin with. They were completely wrong for each other.

When Brad noticed him, he walked over. "Hey Trevor. How are you?"

"Fine, Brad. What's going on?"

"Just finished giving finals. I was going to reward myself with a milkshake. Mind if I join you?"

A little surprised by the request, Trevor motioned to the empty side of the booth. He shouldn't be so suspicious. It was a friendly town.

"Hey, Joy. Could you get me a vanilla milkshake, please?"

"Coming right up, Brad," Joy said as she brought Trevor another hot chocolate.

Brad looked over at Trevor. "Everyone's excited about the big parade. Everything's set, I imagine."

"As far as can be expected, yes." They spoke for a few minutes about the big event. Trevor took a sip of his chocolate, enjoying the rich, creamy taste.

Brad chuckled. "Yeah, they make the best hot chocolate in town here. I think they get their chocolate by special order. Thanks, Joy," Brad said as a large creamy shake was placed in front of him. He stirred the beverage with his straw, clearly hesitating about something.

Trevor watched him. Now, he was no detective, but it seemed to him that Brad wasn't merely making a neighborly visit. Trevor wrapped his hands around his cup and said, "Something on your mind, Brad?"

He looked up, his eyes big behind his glasses. "Is it that obvious?"

Trevor grinned. "Go ahead. I'm listening."

With a big sigh, Brad said, "I'm worried about Mary."

Now Trevor was uneasy. Had Mary been wrong about their relationship? Was Brad expecting more and had heard rumors about him and Mary? "What do you mean?"

Brad took a big sip of his shake and hummed in approval. "Boy, that's good." As if buoyed by the treat, he looked Trevor straight in the eyes and said, "I don't want you to hurt her.

Trevor was uncomfortable and shifted in his seat. "I'm not sure I understand what you mean."

"Come on, Trevor. I may be a nerd. I may be distracted, but one thing I'm not and that's stupid. I know that Mary's attracted to you and that's her choice. But she's special and I don't want to see her heart broken."

Trevor sat back in the booth. "Okay." His eyes shot to Brad's. "Do you have feelings for her?"

"Of course I do. She's a special friend. Always has been and always will be. She helped me see a better side of myself, a more valuable side. She's never made fun of me or worse ignored me. Believe me, I've had enough of that to last several lifetimes. Mary let me know it was okay to be me.

"Now, before you read anything into that, let me say that I love her. As a friend. But as a friend I won't stand by and let someone mistreat her." Brad sighed. "Tell me you're not some jerk who's going to give her a special Christmas and then pack it up, never to be heard from again."

Trevor thought for a moment. "Mary's real lucky to have you in her corner." Brad said nothing but continued to stare at him. "The, ah, attraction is there for me too. I . . . well, to be perfectly honest with you, I'm in love with her." It actually felt good to say it. He frowned and added, "But there are . . . complications that I don't know how we'll overcome."

"Her parents," Brad said, taking another sip.

"That's right. You've seen it too?"

"Yeah." Brad shook his head. "Mary's got to get past this huge feeling of responsibility she has. Ever since I've known her, she's been taking care of her father, almost like a nursemaid, hovering. Since her mother's shown up, it's like her entire purpose in life revolves around them."

"Exactly. I've been trying to tell her that."

They both drank in the silence, thinking their own thoughts. Trevor looked up and said, "All right, you're the smart one. Any suggestions on how to get her past this?"

Brad considered the question. "My first thought would be to get her away from them. But how you do that, I have no idea."

Trevor did. There was an answer to getting Mary away from the craziness of her parents' marriage. He had to get Merrilyn and Frank to confront the issues in their marriage and decide things for themselves. And he had to step aside for Mary to take over the events business. His mind got busy with a plan, knowing it would probably mean the end of his association with Kennedy Swenson Events.

And the end of their relationship.

Chapter Fifteen

Hal's Place was a madhouse. It seemed that everyone in Central Florida had decided to visit the diner today. Like any business owner, Grace was happy for the revenue, but how was she supposed to get ready for the Swenson's party tonight if she didn't have a moment to herself?

Mac had been quiet this morning when they'd shared an early morning cup of coffee before opening the diner. No doubt his mind had been on what was going on in New York. The book deal his agent was working on was coming to a head and could go either way. It had Mac nervous as a cat.

After giving directions to a family from Ohio, clearing a large table of friends from Miami, and checking out a few of the local children buying Christmas candy, she was ready for a break. But another party came in and she glanced around, wondering where she was going to sit them.

A few minutes later, Mac and Pauline entered the dining room, strange expressions on both their faces. It made Grace worry. Had something happened?

He joined her at the cash register and waited until she'd given change to a happy customer. "Grace, we need to talk."

She glanced around at the full restaurant. "A little busy right now, honey. Can't it wait?"

"No." He placed a hand lightly on her shoulder. "Pauline will take over. Come on, let's go to the office."

Her stomach was in knots as they walked. The knots tightened when he locked the office door behind them. "What is it?"

A smile brightened Mac's face, so large that she thought she might need sunglasses.

"I got it, Grace. The four-book deal. Just like I wanted." He laughed out loud, shaking his head. "Everything I asked for, they gave me. Can you believe it?" He pulled her into his arms and swung her around.

She lost her breath and then giggled, hugging him tightly. "I'm very proud of you, Mac. You deserve it, you really do."

He stopped spinning and just held her, exhaling loud and long. "Thanks, honey. I wanted it. I wanted it so bad, Grace. It's a dream come true for a photographer."

"I know. They couldn't have given the contract to a better photographer." She took his face in her hands and kissed him tenderly. After a dreamy moment, he took control of the kiss and before long, they were both breathless.

Mac rested his forehead against hers. "I was afraid to want it so much. I guess that's silly."

"No, it's not. It's a nice Christmas present for you."

His hands went to her shoulders and he massaged. "Yeah. Um, I've got to get started in January. Pauline and I have started mapping out my trip."

Her heart dropped and her throat grew heavy. "January. One week."

"Yeah, but we'll have Christmas together. And New Years. Although . . ."

She stepped back. "What?"

"I'll need to make a quick trip to New York. You know, get the ball dropping at midnight. It's iconic. It really needs to be in the books, because—"

"I realize it's iconic, Mac. You don't need to explain." She moved away to glance out the window, sadness flooding her soul.

"Now Grace, this is a good thing."

She swung around, tears escaping her eyes. "Is it? You think it's a good thing to leave for a year? To be away from your wife?"

"We'll see each other." He walked to her and rubbed her arms. "I'll come back and you'll come to me. The time will go fast, really."

"Mac. A year."

"Grace. When will I ever get this opportunity again? We're riding the waves of *Christmas In America*. This four-book deal has the possibility of being really big. It won't affect our marriage, I promise."

"How can you promise that? How can it not? You'll be working all over the country. I'll be here running Hal's Place."

"But we'll—"

"Don't say we'll see each other. You'll be deep in your work, having the time of your life, treated to four-star hotels and room service." Tears streamed down her cheek. "I know you deserve it, you've worked hard. But I can't believe you'll be thinking of a little town in Central Florida or of your . . . your . . . plain ol' wife." She wiped her cheeks with the back of her hand and moved to the door.

"Grace—"

She stopped and whirled around. "I guess the thing that hurts most is that you're jumping at the opportunity to be away from me."

"That's ridiculous!"

"I've got to get back to work. You can get back to your planning. Just remember we're expected at the Swenson's party tonight. *If* you've got time for it." She couldn't face him anymore. Before she collapsed into a weeping heap, she hurried out, stopping by the restroom to splash cold water over her face.

Was she overreacting? Probably, but she couldn't help it. She already missed Mac. A whole year. She sighed loudly.

She patted her cheeks dry with a paper towel and took a deep breath. There were customers to serve and she was determined to give them a wonderful experience at Hal's.

So, she'd get back to running the restaurant. And not think of her husband leaving her in January.

The Swenson estate twinkled like a fairytale castle. Mary's mother had outdone herself with the décor. The entrance to the house was lit with small white lights that welcomed guests to the festivities. The back patio was adorned with lanterns draped in Christmas greenery. Small candles cradled in the center of poinsettia wreaths glided across the swimming pool.

The inside of the house was a Norman Rockwell picture with a fire in the fireplace, Christmas music quietly playing, a large tree glowing, and greenery tastefully displayed everywhere.

It seemed the entire town had shown up for the Swenson's Christmas party. Merrilyn was obviously thrilled. She glided between guests as the lady of the manor, with the skills that came naturally to her.

Mary hung back, a glass of wine in her hand, and watched. As her mother went from guest to guest, and her father shared a laugh with a few men, she realized that it would be harder than she thought to get them together.

Her father looked so handsome tonight. She'd laid out his suit herself, wanting him to look his absolute best.

She saw Trevor enter and her heart skipped a beat. He really was gorgeous. She took a sip of wine to cool her dry throat and watched him. He greeted a few people he knew and looked around. Who was he looking for?

When his eyes found hers, she knew. She smiled as he sauntered over, his eyes never leaving hers.

"Nice party," he said, grinning at her.

"You know my mother." She enjoyed the full body scan that he gave her, and tried not to shiver.

"You look beautiful."

She was breathless as she looked into his gleaming green eyes. At that moment she wanted to go with him, anywhere, just to be alone.

Then he smiled at her and she wanted to curl up into his lap forever.

"Mary, darling, what are you doing hiding over here," Merrilyn said as she took Mary's arm. She merely glanced at Trevor. Since the scene in the den last Saturday, Mary had noticed that her mother's interactions with Trevor had become cool at best.

"Come on, sweetheart, I'd like you to meet a new investor your father invited. From New York but winters in Florida." The snub to Trevor was clear. Mary looked over her shoulder and smiled sadly at Trevor as her mother hurried her away.

"Mr. Winters, here's my lovely daughter, Mary. Frank, why haven't you introduced them before?"

"It must have been an oversight," he said finishing his drink, giving his daughter an apologetic grin for Merrilyn's interference.

"So happy to meet you, Mr. Winters," Mary said and then was distracted by the appearance of their housekeeper, Susan Appleby, entering the room.

The fortyish, attractive woman who normally cleaned house in jeans and tee shirt, appearing in a black dress, white apron, and tiny white hat was just too funny as Mary and Frank looked at each other and tried to keep from laughing. Frank suddenly had to cough and Mary sniffed into a napkin trying to hide her mirth.

"Hors d'oeuvres?" the woman said, holding out a tray, a tight smile straining her face.

"Thank you, Mrs. Appleby," Merrilyn said sharply. After Frank and Mr. Winters took slices of melon wrapped in prosciutto she added, "There are other guests."

"Yes ma'am." Mrs. Appleby gave a last pleading look at Frank and Mary and then took the tray around the room, causing the two to squelch more laughter.

Frank cleared his throat. "Was the uniform necessary, Merry?"

"Yes, it was," she snapped. "Is there some reason you don't want *Mrs.* Appleby to be a server here tonight?"

"I hate to see her in such a subservient position. She's more like one of the family."

"And how does *Mr.* Appleby feel about that?"

"Oh, Mrs. Appleby's a widow Mom," Mary interjected.

Merrilyn's face seemed to pale. "Oh. I see." Then her eyes started to flare as she looked at her husband. "And just what has been going on since I've been gone, Frank? Right here in my own house."

Frank started coughing, causing Mr. Winters to slap him on the back. "You all right?"

Frank stopped a passing waiter and took a glass of wine. He gave one look at Merrilyn and then drank the entire glass at once. "Merry. I think you owe me an apology."

"I owe you an apology?" Merrilyn huffed out a laugh. "I owe *you* an apology? I'm still waiting for one from five years ago."

"What—"

"I, ah, think I'll just mingle, Frank," Mr. Winters said. Apparently he could see a storm brewing, one he didn't want any part of. "Nice to meet you, Ms. Swenson," he said to Mary before leaving. Quickly.

"Did you see that? Frank, you're driving away potential suitors for your daughter."

"Suitors?" Now it was Mary's turn to choke.

"Merry. I'm going to let our daughter choose her own companions. Unless you'd like to lose your relationship with her, I'd suggest that you do the same."

Mary was embarrassed that her father's voice had risen. She glanced around seeing that others were looking in their direction. "You guys," she whispered through clenched teeth. "Could we possibly have this argument later? We do have guests."

Her parents separated, leaving her standing there alone and miserable. Things were not going well. What should she do now? Seeing Mrs. Appleby, she headed over. She smiled and reached for an appetizer, a spinach parmesan ball. Motioning to the housekeeper's starched uniform she said, "I'm really sorry about this. Mom's just . . . you know, really formal at times."

The housekeeper patted her arm. "It's all right. I understand." Leaning closer, she whispered, "But why does she hate me?"

Mary didn't want to tell her that her mother suspected she and her father were involved. It was ridiculous. Especially since Mrs. Appleby was engaged to a really nice sub-contractor that Frank had introduced her to.

Seeing the woman waiting for an answer, Mary said, "She . . . just has a hard time warming up to people sometimes." *Especially if she sees them as competition.*

Mrs. Appleby hurried away and Mary looked over the crowd. She saw Grace off to the side, nursing a glass of wine, looking despondent.

Mary walked to her side. "Hey. Why the frown?"

"Huh? Oh, no reason. I mean no new reason." She took a sip and then looked across the room. "Same old reason."

Mary's eyes followed hers. Mac stood with several couples by the doors leading outside. His lips were smiling but his eyes were not. He had a hollow expression. Mary knew he was probably just as depressed as his wife.

"What happened?" she asked.

Grace took a deep sip of her drink. "He signed the papers. It's a done deal. Mac's contracted to do a new series. *Spring In America, Summer In America*, etc." She sighed heavily. "He'll be on the road for virtually the whole next year." Tears filled her eyes as she whispered, "He couldn't say no."

Mary felt a lump in her throat. Her eyes filled as well as she put her arm around her friend. She wasn't sure what to say, how to comfort her friend. "Is there anything I can do?"

Grace shook her head, her gaze down. "I probably shouldn't have come tonight. I'm not really in the holiday mood."

"Regardless, I'm glad you're here. And I bet Mac is as well." Mary squeezed her friend's arm. "If he's going to be traveling, don't you think you should make the most of your time together?"

Grace glanced over at her husband. "Maybe. I just can't get past the hurt that he'd rather be on the road than with me."

"That's just nonsense. He's crazy in love with you, everyone knows that."

Shaking her head again, she said, "I'm not so sure anymore." Before the tears fell, Grace ran for the powder room.

Mary was deflated. Some holiday party this was turning out to be.

And it was just beginning.

When Big Jed came out of the kitchen wearing an ancient tuxedo with Elena in a party dress, on his arm, Mary was sure that her mother would have a fit.

"Elena! What are you doing here? I'm sure you're needed in the kitchen," Merrilyn said trying to smile as she said it.

"Mr. Swenson say I can attend party with Jed. Your husband is nice man."

"Excuse us, Merry," Big Jed said escorting Elena into the party.

Mary saw the fire in her mother's eyes and quickly went to her. "Mom. Take a breath," she warned and stayed with her as she tried to calm down.

"Merrilyn. Look who showed up?"

Both women turned to see Trevor standing with a distinguished looking man, mid-fifties, his salt and pepper hair stylishly fashioned, and smiling warmly at Merrilyn.

Mary saw her mother light up. "Why Benjamin, darling. I didn't expect to see you here." She reached out and kissed the man on both cheeks. Remembering her manners, Merrilyn took the man's arm and said, "Sweetheart, this is Benjamin Crandall. A business associate of mine. We're planning his big Valentine's Day bash in Manhattan. Benjamin, my daughter Mary Swenson."

Benjamin took Mary's hand to his lips. "Very nice to meet you. You're as lovely as your mother."

"Thank you," she said without smiling. "My father thinks so as well."

"But darling, why didn't you tell me you were coming? I could have set aside a whole day to confer with you."

"I wanted to surprise you. When Trevor called and invited me to your party, I thought it would be great fun."

"Trevor invited you?" Mary said, her eyes turning to the man in question.

"I, ah, thought it would be good business. Since Mr. Crandall was only a few hours away in Palm Beach." His eyes didn't waver from Mary's.

"And who is this?" Frank's booming voice grabbed the foursome's attention.

"Frank, this is Benjamin Crandall, from New York and Palm Beach. Benjamin, Frank Swenson."

"Her husband," Mary inserted.

Frank's eyes hardened. "Funny. I didn't know that Merry would be inviting one of her boyfriends to the party."

Benjamin frowned. "I'm afraid I've just met your charming daughter."

"He means me," Merrilyn said. "He calls me Merry. Short for Merrilyn."

"It's my father's pet name for my mother," Mary couldn't help adding.

Trevor took Mary's arm firmly and led her a few feet away from the group. "Why don't we walk out on the patio, let them handle this," he said in her ear. "It's none of our business."

"How can my parents' lives be none of my business?" Mary replied in her defense. "And what's the big idea inviting this handsome but predatory male here to show up my father. No offense, Mr. Crandall," she directed to Benjamin.

He lifted his brows. "None taken?"

Frank piped up. "Show up your father? When pigs fly! Not a ghost of a chance that some fancy looking man with overpriced clothes and over-styled hair will show me up. No hard feelings, Crandall," he said to Benjamin.

"Of course not?" The man was clearly confused.

The sound of knocking on a door could be heard over the conversations in the room. "Grace! Grace, honey, come on out. Can't we talk about this?"

Grace reappeared, at the edges of the room, a tissue in her hand. "I can't think of anything to say."

"How about 'I love you and support you'? That'd be nice."

"Merry, I want to know and I want to know now. Is something going on with you and this man?"

"Me!" Merrilyn motioned toward the unsuspecting Mrs. Appleby, who was walking past them. "Are you and your *housekeeper* having fun playing house?"

"Mom! That's terrible. Why Mrs. Appleby is the nicest person and incidentally she has a—"

"Leave it alone, Mary," Trevor said, taking her arm and trying to lead her away. "Let. Them. Talk."

Mary yanked her arm away. "Since you've been here you've done nothing but diminish any chance for my parents to get back together. I thought you were on my side, that maybe we . . . that you cared. About my family, about . . . me."

"Of course I care. I care too much, when I should be thinking about myself, whether I'll have a job come the new year. I don't know if I'll be getting any kind of bonus, which my family happens to be counting on. And no matter what I do, I'll probably lose the only girl I've ever been in love with. What infuriates me is it's all because you can't cut those apron strings, sweetheart, and live your own life! You can't see the highly talented, beautiful woman that you are. You're hanging here with your daddy, using him and your mother as an excuse for not living your own life.

"Well, that's it for me. I'm not standing around waiting for all this to work out. I'll email my resignation tomorrow." He glared at Frank and Merrilyn. "You two should be locked in some room and left there until you decide if you want to stay married to each other or not. Make a decision, for God's sake."

He turned to Mary and said, "Grow up and have your own life, Mary with an 'a' one 'r.' Whatever, wherever, and with whomever that may be."

Everyone in the room had quieted, listening to Trevor's rant. He didn't seem to care in the least, but stormed to the front door, stopping in front of Mac and Grace. "And you two. The answer is so obvious. Grace, take a year off and travel with your husband. You have good people to run the diner; you have nothing holding you back. Do you know how many people would love to have the chance to travel around the country with the person they love? Take the opportunity now, while you can."

He gave Mary a last glance and then turned and left.

The room stayed silent for another moment until Big Jed said, "I guess sometimes it just takes a Yankee to say what's what." The crowd chuckled and went back to their conversations.

Mary was torn between wanting to go after Trevor to argue that he was wrong and wanting to go some place quiet and think about what he'd said.

Merrilyn and Frank stood glaring at each other, neither speaking. Finally, Frank muttered under his breath, "Mrs. Appleby's looking better and better." He headed to the door, grabbing his jacket. "Please excuse me," he said to the those around him as he started out.

"Dad!" Mary called, which did no good.

How could everything have turned out so wrong? This was supposed to be the night they reunited. They were supposed to remember how much they enjoyed being together, entertaining together.

And Trevor. Her heart sank knowing that he was probably planning his departure at that moment. She'd never see him again.

Suddenly all the silliness of her parents' marriage was nothing compared to the thought of losing him.

Chapter Sixteen

Light filtered into the bedroom causing Mary's face to heat. She cracked one eye to see that it was early morning. She sat up and looked around. Her mind tried to settle and remember why she was sleeping on a lounge chair in her mother's bedroom.

She wished she could forget.

The previous night had been horrible. After Trevor and Frank left, the guests started streaming out as well. Her mother had held up the best she could, but when the last person left, she broke down and sobbed uncontrollably.

Mary hadn't had the chance for that quiet reflection on what Trevor had said. She'd spent hours holding Merrilyn, bringing her tea, listening to her vent about what a mess she'd made of her life.

But all the while Mary thought about Trevor. And the fact that she wasn't so different from her mother.

Mary looked at the bed to see her mother still sleeping. Good. She really wasn't ready for act two of "How My Life Is Terrible," Merry Swenson edition.

She got up and went downstairs into the kitchen to brew a pot of coffee. As she watched the pot, she thought again about what Trevor had said. Was she living her life for her parents? Was she so lacking in self-confidence, so afraid of living her own life?

If it weren't for that darn parade, she'd just head out to Bermuda, alone if necessary. That didn't sound too bad. In fact, it sounded pretty good. The only thing that would make it better would be if she were heading to Bermuda with Trevor.

The aroma of the dark liquid had her mind clearing and her senses settling. She poured herself a cup and doctored it just the way she liked. She heard a sound behind her and turned to see her mother entering. Crying again. How could a person have so many tears inside of them?

Letting out a sigh, Mary fixed a cup of coffee for her. They both sat down at the breakfast table and she was glad when Merrilyn stopped sobbing long enough to take a sip.

"He didn't come home last night, Mary," she whispered.

"What? Dad?"

"Yes. I peeked into his room and the bed was still made. He stayed out all night." She started sniffing again. "Probably partying with Mrs. Applebeeeee!" The tears stared in earnest then. And Mary wrapped an arm around her."

"Come on, Mom. No more tears, okay? How about we straighten up the great room. That'll get your mind off . . . ah, things."

Merrilyn shrugged without any interest. "Might as well." They walked to the kitchen as Merrilyn said, "Did I ever tell you about the night you were conceived?"

Oh, Good Lord, no! "That's all right, Mom," she said patting Merrilyn's arm. "No need to . . . What's going on here?"

The great room was disorganized and messy, a result of last night's party. But that wasn't what caught Mary's attention. Sprawled out on one couch was Frank Swenson, hand over his eyes, snoring. And on another couch was Trevor Crane, lying on his stomach, face smashed into the cushions, one arm hitting the floor.

Mary looked at her mother who was just as confused as she. They walked to the couches and stared at the sleeping men. "What do you suppose happened to them?"

Merrilyn leaned down to Frank's face and then quickly moved away waving a hand. "He smells like a distillery."

Mary followed her mother's example. Trevor's face was hidden so she gently touched his shoulder. He shifted and Mary found herself inches from his face. The fumes were so bad that she fell back on her rear. "They're drunk!"

"Well, that just clinches it." Merrilyn leaned over her husband and poked him. "Frank. Frank. Get up."

"Hmm? What? Somebody there?" Owwwww." Frank said when he started to lift his head.

"Feeling under the weather, darling?" Merrilyn said sweetly.

"Yeah, sweetheart, how about bringing me a few aspirin? And a cup of coffee."

"When pigs fly!" She grabbed a pillow and started pounding on Frank who moaned in agony.

Mary crossed her arms and said, "Dad. I believe explanations are in order, don't you?"

He pulled the pillow out of Merrilyn's hands and said, "I left here last night and needed to cool off. I stopped at the Tavern and Trevor was already. We commiserated and . . . I'm afraid had a little too much to drink. He couldn't find his hotel key so Sven, the bartender, brought us home." He tried to grin. "I couldn't exactly make it up the stairs.

"You're imbeciles, the lot of you!" Merrilyn cried.

"Could you guys keep it quiet? I'm dying here," Trevor said in a gravelly voice.

Mary turned to him, her heart racing in apprehension. "I thought you'd be in New York by now."

Trevor eased up into a sitting position, blinked at her, and rubbed the side of his head. "Yeah. That was the plan until I remembered I probably wouldn't be able to get a flight out because of the holidays." He leaned over his legs and said, "Besides. I said I'd be available to help with parade if needed. Then I'll leave. You won't have to see me again. Ms. Swenson."

Mary felt a pain in her heart. She'd really and truly lost him. The right man finally comes along and she's too busy interfering in her parents' lives to notice.

She sat beside him on the couch. Just as she was trying to think of something to say, her mother said, "This finishes it, Frank. I left after one of our parties, now I guess we'll get divorced after one of our parties."

Mary wanted so much to say something but decided for once to be quiet. She bit her tongue hard to remind herself.

Frank stared at Merrilyn. He blinked a couple of times and then said, "Okay, fine. Divorce me. But before you do, I think I have the right to know why you left in the first place."

"Like you don't know."

Wearily he said, "Merry, for the life of me, I really don't. Tell me."

"Perhaps we should leave," Trevor said starting to stand.

"No. Stay," Merrilyn commanded. Her eyes burning Frank's she said. "Let me refresh your memory, darling. New Year's Eve. Five years ago. Our house was filled with friends, family, business associates. It was a wonderful party. At least it was until just after midnight."

When she didn't go on, Frank said, "Okay. Just after midnight . . ."

"At midnight everyone kissed as is the tradition. There had been a problem in the kitchen so I came out during the countdown. I couldn't find you."

Merrilyn worried her fingers together, very uncharacteristic. "We'd both been so busy that year. Me with my volunteer activities and you with work. You were working all the time, I was afraid . . . well, anyway, I'd decided that the New Year would be a beginning for us. I wanted to show that to you by giving you a big kiss at midnight.

"Everyone was yelling and cheering and kissing but I still didn't see you. I walked down the hall and heard a noise coming from your office. I looked in the room and . . ." Tears leaked from Merrilyn's eyes. Pain, betrayal, disappointment filled her face.

"Go on, Merry. What did you see?" Frank asked.

Confusion was now added to the emotions on her face. "You really want me to say?"

"Merry, all I remember about that night was that Jenkins, my former superintendent, brought a couple of bottles of whiskey, which he shared with everyone." His brows furrowed, and he moaned. "Is that what upset you? That I had too much to drink?"

"No, that you were kissing Mrs. Jenkins on top of your desk! That's what upset me!"

"What?"

"Not even just a little 'Happy New Year' kiss. You two were in a passionate embrace, kissing deeply."

"Dad!" Mary was sick to her stomach. All her beliefs about her father were questioned at that moment. Trevor tried to put a hand on her shoulder but she flung it off. "I can't believe you! Here all this time I've stood by you, thinking you were the wronged party. But now I find out that you brought it on yourself? How could you?"

"Mary," her father implored.

"Well, Frank. You've not only ruined our marriage, you've hurt our daughter. Good job."

Before they could get sidetracked, Frank turned to his wife. "I can't believe you saw what you thought you saw. It's just crazy talk. I would never, ever cheat on you. In fact, I've been in love with you since the first day I saw you and I will until the day I die."

"Then why were you kissing that woman?"

"Merry, I don't know." He rubbed his head. "I don't remember any of that. Are you sure about what you saw?"

"That's your excuse? That I imagined what I know I saw? What I want to know is how long had it been going on between the two of you? Why didn't you pursue her once I left?"

"Because there's never been another woman for me, Merry! How can I make you believe it?"

"You can't. I remember getting ready for that party. I tried to have all your favorite party foods there. I had my hair down and full, just the way you liked. I had a dress made special, one that I thought you'd like."

"It was blue," Frank said softly.

"Yes it was, sky blue, your favorite. And then you betrayed me, in my own house. How could you? I . . . I . . ." The tears were flowing now as Merrilyn fled from the room, saying, "I can't do this anymore."

"Mom! Wait!" Mary followed her giving a glare toward her father.

Frank sighed loud and long. He turned to Trevor and said, "I swear I don't remember any of that. Let that be a lesson to you, son. Never wise to drink too much."

Trevor chuckled at the absurdity of the situation and then swore at himself for causing more head pain. He stood and wobbled, trying to take a few steps, and then fell back onto the couch, lying back with a moan.

Slapping Trevor's knee, Frank said, "Oh, Trevor Crane, look at the two of us. Sitting her nursing hangovers while the women we love have given up on us. What are we going to do?"

Trevor rubbed his aching head. "No clue. You're older. Aren't you supposed to be wiser?"

"You'd think." Frank leaned back and mirrored Trevor's pose."You know what the problem is, don't you?" he asked.

Trevor smirked. "Apparently not."

"The problem is that we've been letting these women run our lives. We've become pitiful victims to their moods and irrational beliefs."

"Hmm." Trevor was half-listening, hoping for a moment of relief.

Frank sat up, suddenly. "I think that's it, Trevor, my boy. We've got to take back control of the situation. I'm tired of being Merry's whipping boy. It's time I let my wife know that I am not giving up on us. And too bad if she doesn't like it."

Trevor began to warm up to Frank's little speech. He sat up feeling his brain start to function again. "You sure about this, Frank?"

"I . . . think so. Look, my letting Merry have time to cool off didn't work. We've wasted five years on that idea. I'm tired of being alone. I'm going to go get her. What do you think?"

"Yeah." Trevor was into it now. "Go for it, Frank."

Frank narrowed his eyes at Trevor. "What about you? You gonna give up on my Mary? Let the best thing that'll probably ever happen to you get away?"

Trevor thought about it for half a second. His eyes softened as he said, "No. I love Mary."

Smiling, Frank said, "I'll be sure you get that bonus." He winked at Trevor.

"Thanks. Really." Trevor took a breath and said, "So what do we do?"

"I'm not sure. But we've got today and tomorrow to fix things before Christmas." His eyes looked off into the distance. "First thing, I've got to set the record straight about that New Year's Eve party."

Trevor sincerely wished Frank the best of luck. He knew he'd need his own luck to win back Mary.

Mary was trying to work. "Trying" being the operative word, as it was her last day before closing her doors for the Christmas holidays. No one had been more ready for a day to be over.

There were no tickets to Bermuda or any tropical island now. The best she could do was to load up her car and head for Cocoa Beach, an hour away. There was no way she was going to stay for any more drama from her parents. She pinched between her eyes to ease the tension.

She heard her door open and looked up from her desk to see her mother approaching. Merrilyn's face was tight, her eyes red. No surprise.

"Hi, Mom."

"Sweetheart." Merrilyn nervously rubbed the straps of her purse as if trying to build up courage.

"Did you need something?" Mary asked solemnly.

Merrilyn took a chair in the reception area and tried to meet her daughter's eyes. "I just wanted to say that . . . I'm sorry for bringing you into this."

Mary looked back down to continue her work. "Forget about it."

"No, I can't. You see, I was just so devastated five years ago, that I wasn't thinking straight. I ran away and hoped that your father would come after me." In a childlike voice she added, "He didn't."

Mary set her pen down and took a breath. "Mom. You don't need to be sorry for anything. I wish I had been a little more understanding with you. I mean, since I know what happened now."

Merrilyn dropped her head. "I suppose five years is plenty of time to wait for him to come after me. I . . . I think I should start divorce proceedings."

Mary's stomach tied into a painful knot. It was a child's worse nightmare, to hear a parent speak of divorce. Even when the child was an adult. She felt hot tears searing the backs of her eyes.

A part of her yearned to implore her mother not to do it, but remembering Trevor's words, understanding those words, she realized that she had to take the first step to break away from her parents. They had to live their own lives, make their own decisions. She was going to love her parents no matter what. She was going to build her life on her own terms.

And she was going to confidently pursue what she really wanted.

So, she purposefully made her face strong. "Do what you have to do, Mom."

The door opened again and Mary watched an attractive caramel blonde woman step into the office. "Excuse me. I'm looking for Mary Swenson."

Mary stood and approached the woman. "That's me. Can I help you?"

"Yes." The middle-aged woman seemed uncomfortable. She gave a shaky smile and said, "I'm looking for your mother. It's imperative that I speak with her. Do you happen to know where I could find her?"

Merrilyn slowly stood. "Karen?"

"Merry?" The woman's face broke into a smile as she reached out her hand. "It's so good to see you." When Merrilyn cautiously took the hand

and lifted her chin, the woman added, "Although you probably don't feel the same."

"Sweetheart," Merrilyn said to Mary. "I'd like you to meet Karen Jenkins. Wife of your father's former superintendent. I believe I've mentioned her before."

Mary was at a loss for words. She gave the woman a nod and then wondered how to diffuse this explosive situation.

"May I sit down?" Karen Jenkins asked of Mary.

"Yes, of course. Would you like a cold drink? Coffee?"

"No, thank you." Karen sat and nervously fingered the strap of her purse. "Merry, I was wondering if I could speak to you. Privately."

"No need for that," Merrilyn said with a brittle smile. "My daughter knows all about that last New Year's Eve party at my house. What did you want to speak about?"

"That's it exactly. The New Year's Eve party. I understand some things have been misunderstood."

"I don't see how, as I know what I saw— you and my husband kissing."

Karen shook her head. "No. It wasn't like that at all. You see . . ." She stopped to take a breath and obviously choose her words. "Lon and I had been having marital troubles. I didn't even want to go to the party but he insisted. Said it was good for his career." She snickered at that. "He even let me buy a new dress for the party. The prettiest blue thing you ever saw."

Mary saw her mother tense. She reached over and took her hand, which was ice cold. "Go on," Mary said.

Lon stood by me all night, doting on me, making over me. I thought maybe he was changing. Maybe he was making our marriage a priority now. He even kissed me under the mistletoe you had hanging by the back door." Karen smiled.

"It was coming on midnight and he said let's find us an empty room or a closet to bring in the year right. Well, part of me was appalled at the thought. I mean, how shameful. In someone else's house during a party. But another part of me craved the attention from my husband. So, I agreed." She sighed and added, "I didn't realize he was drunk at the time.

"I walked down the hallway just after midnight looking for him. Before I knew what had happened I was pulled into a room and covered with kisses. Well, I thought it was Lon. I knew he'd been drinking his special whiskey and that's what I smelled. I closed my eyes and just . . . you know, enjoyed it.

"But then he started muttering 'Merry.' When I opened my eyes and saw that it was your Frank, I couldn't believe it. I pushed out of his grip and left the room."

Karen's eyes implored Merrilyn. "You've got to believe me, Merry. I didn't know. I never would have been in that room kissing your husband. And Frank thought I was you. I was so embarrassed that I rushed Lon to the car and drove home. I had no idea that you saw that."

"I see," Merrilyn said quietly. "And you never spoke about this with Frank?"

"I didn't see the need. I figured he was as drunk as Lon. Anyway, Frank fired Lon for drinking on the job a couple of weeks later. We divorced not long after that."

Merrilyn's face softened. "Oh, I'm so sorry."

Karen shook her head. "It was the whiskey. He couldn't control it. I guess some can't. Anyway, Frank called me this morning and explained the situation."

"He called you?" Merrilyn asked with one eyebrow raised.

"He had to search to find my number, Merry, honest. I haven't spoken with him since that party. But I felt terrible when he said you'd witnessed what happened. Really, he loves you. It was nothing more than mistaken identity."

A moment passed as Mary watched her mother process this information. She held her breath, waiting.

Then Merrilyn reached out to take Karen's hand. "It was nice of you to come by and explain things to me. I appreciate it."

Karen smiled broadly, making her face appear quite younger. "You're very welcome." She squeezed Merrilyn's hand before releasing it to stand. "I think I've taken up enough of your time. I'll be going now."

Mary walked her to the door. Softly, she said, "Karen. It meant a lot to us for you to come here today. If there's ever anything that you need, please let the Swenson family know."

"Thank you."

It was quiet when the door closed behind Karen Jenkins. Mary could not even begin to guess what her mother was feeling.

Before she could say anything, Merrilyn stood and said, "How is everything coming with the parade? Any final details to attend to?"

"Mom, what about what Karen just told you."

"Yes, I'm relieved to hear that. And disappointed in myself that I didn't have the courage to face your father five years ago and find out the truth." Merrilyn's shoulders slumped slightly as she said, "He didn't come after me, Mary. How can he really love me if he didn't come after me?"

Mary sighed deeply. "I'm afraid we've both pushed the men we love away. I'm not so sure they even know we want them to come after us."

Realization must have come to Merrilyn, because she stepped to Mary and hugged her hard. "Ah, Mary, my darling. I've been such a blind, ignorant, old fool. Too wrapped up in my own problems to see that you were falling in love with Trevor." She kissed Mary's cheek. "I used to dream about the day you'd find your Prince Charming and begin planning your wedding. We'd have such fun with all the details." Merrilyn leaned back, adding, "And he finally comes and I've been so selfish I didn't see it staring me in the face."

"I'm in love with him, Mom."

"I know that, honey."

After a moment of silence, Mary asked, "What did Trevor mean when he spoke about his family needing his bonus?"

Merrilyn rubbed her daughter's back and leaned her head against Mary's. "His father has emphysema. He needs treatment that costs a great deal. I suppose Trevor was counting on the extra money to go to that." Merrilyn sighed. "Again, my selfishness blocked me from seeing Trevor's need."

She took her daughter's face in both her hands. "Trevor's a good man. A bit stubborn at times, just like your father, but he has a good heart. Don't make my mistakes, honey."

"I already have, Mom," she said quietly.

Merrilyn kissed the top of her daughter's head. "You know what?" she said with determination returning to her voice. "I'm finished feeling sorry for myself. I'm tired of my stubborn pride." Her eyes gleamed like a cat. "I want my husband back."

"You do?" Mary said watching her.

"Yes. And you, sweetheart. You have a gorgeous, incredible man that's crazy about you. Are you going to let him get away?"

"I don't know how to stop him."

"Men like to pursue." She smiled at her daughter. "We'll just have to figure out a way to let our men pursue."

"I don't want to be president of your company, Mom." Mary grinned. "But I know of someone who might."

Merrilyn returned the smile. "Yes. I'm inclined to agree with you."

Hope began to take root in Mary's heart. Maybe there was still a chance for her and Trevor. She'd find out soon enough.

Grace and Mac cuddled together on the couch. She'd called in her aunt, Ellen, to take over her shift at the diner so she and Mac could spend the morning talking.

After Trevor's heated suggestion of the night before, they'd left the party, neither speaking on the way home. His idea was simple but with lots of complications. Could she really just take off for a year?

They'd gone into the house and prepared for bed, still silent. As she was pulling down the covers, Mac faced her across the bed and fisted his hands at his hips. "Why not? Why can't you go with me?"

Her throat grew heavy. "You really want me to?"

"Honey." He crawled across the bed and pulled her down with him, holding her tightly. "I always want you with me, don't you know that?" He gently pushed back a strand of her hair.

"I was afraid . . . I was afraid that you . . . well, were getting tired of me. And this was your opportunity for a break from our marriage."

He had the audacity to chuckle. It would have made her mad, but he quickly calmed her. "My darling Grace. Don't you know you're a part of me? You're my heart and soul. Every moment I'm away from you I feel something missing. You complete me like no one or nothing ever could. Even photography."

Her heart swelled with love for him. "Oh, Mac."

"Yes, this is an incredible opportunity. But one reason I want to do it so much is for us. With the money from these books, I'm set. I won't have to travel for business ever again, unless *we* want to. We'll be able to do things here in Charity without worrying about finances. It's for us, baby."

"Mac." She snuggled into his arms and kissed him gently. "I'm so sorry I doubted you. Those are wonderful reasons for doing this. Other than the fact that you'll be brilliant at it."

He chuckled. "Thank you, my biggest fan." His tone grew quiet. "Please go with me, Grace. If need be, we can hire more workers for the diner. Pauline and Ellen can manage. If they want, they can hire more managers. I don't care. As long as you're with me."

Her heart soared. She climbed on top of him and kissed him deeply. Smiling, she said, "Let's start packing."

They'd stayed up most of the night planning, making lists of things to do at the diner, places to go, clothes to pack. Well, that last list was hers.

Now they were enjoying the quiet, just the two of them. Basking in their love for each other. It was pure bliss.

Mac softly kissed her head. "How's the float coming?"

"You mean the Hal's Place Float Float?" They both chuckled. "Good. Mom, Noel, and I have it pretty much ready."

"You know, I'm emceeing the parade." He ran his hand along her arm, bringing a shiver of excitement. "I'd really love to have my wife at my side."

She looked into his brilliant blue eyes and felt her bones melting. "I guess Mom and Noel can handle it. They'll need to get used to me not being around. Since I'll be with you." They kissed again and again.

Mac whispered, "I guess we owe Trevor another free meal."

Chapter Seventeen

The morning of the parade was glorious, with sunshine, a slight breeze, and temperatures hovering over a comfortable seventy-two degrees.

Behind the downtown area of Charity, at the resident's recreational center, it was pandemonium. There were floats of every size and shape, SUV's to pull them, bands, choirs, elves and Santas.

Santas? Mary quickly walked over to the group of Charity senior citizens that would be walking in the parade. All the men had Santa suits while the women were dressed as wives of the jolly man. "Hey, everyone. Didn't we agree that we wouldn't have a bunch of Santas in the parade? You know, confuse the kids?"

"What else we gonna be?" one of the men asked. "Everything was already taken—elves, ornaments, trees, angels—"

"Okay, okay. I get it. Well, try not to be too . . . ah, Santa-ish. Especially since we've got one in a sleigh at the end of the parade."

"Gotcha," the man said and passed the word around. Don't be too Santa-ish.

Mary sighed as she again checked her clipboard, wondering where the Charity Twirlers were since they'd be starting the parade. She looked around and saw Colin, town handyman, stomping by muttering to himself.

"What's wrong, Colin?" Mary asked.

He pointed to a large float in the back and said, "The darn cable company float. Got all them gadgets and now can't get them to work. Typical," he muttered stomping off to get some sort of tool to help them.

She walked past the Presbyterian church choir, all dressed in robes, warming up their voices to sing as they walked the parade. Mary smiled.

Grace and Pauline were busy putting finishing touches on the Hal's Place Float Float. It ended up being cute—a gigantic mug on a flatbed tinted to look as if it held root beer. The top was filled with cotton to resemble whipped cream and a large papier mache cherry crowned the creation.

"Hey!" Grace called out when she spotted Mary. "Get a load of this. Noel, get it cranking." Joy's stepson and employee of Hal's turned a switch and bubbles started coming out of the top of the float.

Mary giggled. "That's wonderful! You've got a bubble maker hidden in the float?"

"Yep." Grace jumped down from the float and went to Mary, giving her a hug.

"It looks awesome. Are you riding with the float, Grace?"

Grace pulled back and said, "No. My fabulous husband is emceeing the parade, remember? I'm going to be up on stage with him." Her smile was heartwarming.

"Everything good then?" Mary asked.

"The best," Grace beamed. "Trevor was absolutely right. After we left the party we talked it all over." She giggled. "And we haven't stopped talking about it. We are so excited about seeing the country together. I can't wait."

Mary wrapped her arm around her friend. "I'm so happy for you."

"Hey Mary! You're needed at Santa's sleigh."

Hearing the call, Mary gave Grace a last hug and then hurried to whatever problem had come up.

She passed the Rotary Club float—a tribute to a Florida Christmas with a melted snowman, elves in Bermuda shorts, lights on palm trees, and water skis with large red bows attached—and gave them the thumbs up.

She passed a local Jazz band warming up, its members dressed like Christmas ornaments, the toy shop's "Santa's Workshop," and the Garden Club with their fleet of toy wagons filled with poinsettias to hand out to spectators.

"What's the trouble?" she asked Little Jed when finally reaching the sleigh.

"Daddy's in a snit because of what you got to pull the sleigh."

Mary looked at the large red Chevy Suburban. "Why? It'll pull the float just fine. We tested it."

"No, not the vehicle. The animals."

Mary glanced at the group of large plastic reindeer that she'd rented to be attached to the sleigh. "Okay, what's wrong with reindeer pulling Santa's sleigh. It kind of seems obvious to me."

"May be. But I thought we were celebrating Charity," Big Jed said approaching the two. "I been in Central Florida all my life and I ain't never seen no reindeer. That's why I wanted the alligators."

Her head started to ache. Mary told herself to calm down, she could fix this. This was Big Jed, she knew how to handle him.

She took a breath and looked him in the eyes. "Big Jed, you are absolutely right. Reindeer aren't usually in Charity." She was pleased to see him grin and nod his head.

"However, there must have been a mix-up. I mean, it's understandable. Most people would expect reindeer pulling Santa's sleigh. And since there's no time to change anything and the kids would be so, so disappointed if you, I mean Santa, didn't show up, how about we just go with it?"

"Well..."

"But I see your point. These reindeer should reflect Central Florida." She lifted her eyebrows.

Both Jeds grinned widely. "I understand what you mean, Mary," Little Jed said. "Give me ten minutes, Daddy. I'll fix it up right."

Satisfied that the reindeer crisis was over, Mary headed back through the floats. One caught her eye and she frowned. Looking down at her clipboard, she couldn't find one that fit the description of the charming little house float, decorated suitably for Christmas.

She walked over and saw Mayor Scott, his wife Ellen, and Brad standing there smiling at her. "What's going on?" she asked.

"What do you think?" the mayor said as he, Ellen, and Brad stepped aside to reveal the title of the float. Mary's eyes grew large as she saw the words:

Swenson Realty
"There's No Place Like Home For The Holidays"

Mary couldn't speak for the lump in her throat. Her eyes roamed over the beautiful float as the Christmas song from the float's title wafted softly through the air.

"I . . . can't believe this. What . . . How . . ."

"It was Trevor's idea," Brad said. "He brought it to the mayor. Said that since you'd spent all your time planning the parade, it was fitting that you have a float celebrating your business."

Mayor Scott jumped in. "And I heartily agreed. We got the town council to pitch in and with my lovely wife's decorating talents, put it together. It's in thanks for all your work, Mary. We wanted you to know how much we appreciate it. And you."

Mary's eyes welled up. What a thoughtful thing for the town to do. She sniffed and said, "Thank you." After giving them all hugs, she walked away before she started bawling.

Trevor. He'd done that for her. He'd been thinking of her. Mary's heart squeezed with love for the man. She wanted so desperately to tell him the things that were in her heart.

A loud blast of trumpets from the high school band brought her mind back. She couldn't do anything until this darn parade was over.

At exactly nine o'clock, Mac McCrae took the microphone in front of Hal's Place and welcomed everyone to the parade. Mary walked over to the podium, confident that everything was in place. She saw Grace happily standing by her husband's side. It made her smile.

The Charity Twirlers started down the street, followed by Boy Scouts. Mary grinned and waved at Holly, who tried to give her a wink and still keep her eyes on her baton.

Mary looked around wondering where her mother and father were? She hadn't seen either since yesterday. She and her mother had spent the afternoon getting makeovers and shopping. Then they'd had a light supper in her apartment.

She hadn't seen her father since finding him in the great room with a hangover. Along with Trevor.

She hadn't seen Trevor, but she was sure he was somewhere around the parade set-up. He said he'd be at the parade and she believed him. She sighed. Still, it would have been nice to actually see him.

Mary quickly bolstered her resolve. She would see him, after the parade. And she would make it known that she was ready to move on. With him, hopefully.

A few of the town's sports teams paraded down the route, waving to the cheering crowd. They were followed by police on horses. Mary enjoyed seeing the gasps and excitement from the children in the crowd.

Pleased with the way the parade was going, she searched the crowd again. Still no Trevor. No parents.

"And coming up now is my personal favorite," Mac said with a chuckle. It's the Hal's Place Float . . . Float." The kids squealed when bubbles came pouring out of the top of the float.

Next came the senior citizens, all Santas and Mrs. Clauses. Mary watched as the children's smiles turned to frowns. She'd been afraid of this. Some kids pointed, others cried, and still others turned to parents asking questions. Yikes!

The leader of the group apparently noticed this because at his signal, all the men lowered their beards, took off their hats, and cried, "Merry Christmas!"

Mary sighed in relief as everyone burst out laughing along with the senior citizens. Crisis averted.

Until the next float, the local cable company, came by, still unable to get anything to work. The crowd chuckled.

Next came the church choral group, the Rotary Float, the high school marching band, another church with a float showcasing the Nativity, the Garden Club elves, and then . . . her float. It was beautiful and made her heart sing. She mouthed the words "Thank you" to Mayor Scott, Ellen, and Brad. And again felt a pang in her heart to speak those words to Trevor.

The striking "Santa's Workshop" float drew "ooh's" and "aah's" from the crowd. Mary was sure that it would be deemed the most beautiful float in the parade. The loud, happy tune of "Santa Claus is Coming to Town" began as the jazz band preceded the man of the hour—well, in this case Big Jed as Santa, along with Elena as Mrs. Claus.

Mary looked closely to see the reindeer, a point of contention, coming into view. And she burst out laughing. Each reindeer had been decked out as any local Floridian or carefree tourist. Each reindeer sported sunglasses. Many wore flowered shirts. One wore a headband of reindeer antlers over his own and another wore a headband with mistletoe on the end. Still another sported a mouse ears cap, a nod to the nearby theme park. A ball cap lauding the local high school was on one reindeer and next to him an Orlando Magic Basketball team cap.

But the best was the lead reindeer, Rudolph. His red nose had been lathered with white suntan lotion.

The crowd howled at the reindeer and applauded madly. With Elena at his side, Big Jed sat in the sleigh, smiling widely, causing Mary to chuckle. When he looked her way, she blew a kiss to him. He winked and let out a thunderous "Ho, ho, ho."

Mary watched the final float pass by with a feeling of deep satisfaction. It had been a tremendous success, partly because of Trevor's help. She stepped down from the stage, determined to find him. She had a few things to say and he was going to listen.

"Hey Mary!" Holly called out from the side. "Wasn't that a fantabulous parade?"

Mary grabbed her cousin and hugged her. "Yes it was." She kissed her nose and added, "And you were one of the reasons why."

"It was fun. But the best part was the reindeer. Do you think they come here on vacation too?"

Mary chuckled. "I wouldn't be surprised." She ruffled Holly's hair and said, "By the way, um, you haven't seen Trevor around have you?"

"Sure. I saw him before the parade started. He said he was checking the parade route to make sure everything was ready."

Her heart lightened at that. "Okay. Good."

Holly frowned. "Then he said to 'break a leg.' Why would he want me to break my leg? Then I couldn't march in the parade."

Mary smothered a smile. "It's an expression, sweetheart. People in the theatre use it before a show to mean 'good luck.'"

"Oh. Really? Well, why didn't he just say 'good luck'?"

"Maybe you can ask him when you see him. Oh, and if you do, would you tell him I'm looking for him?"

"I don't have to," Holly said pointing. "Here he comes now."

Mary's stomach dipped just like a drop in a rollercoaster. She pushed a hand to her middle and slowly turned around, trying to remember the little speech that she'd worked on.

And promptly forgot everything.

He was gorgeous as usual, wearing khakis, white shirt, and navy sports coat. Her throat grew dry.

But his expression shocked her. His eyes shot straight to her, as if they were the only ones on the street. The intensity of his look took her breath away. If she had ever seen a lion on the prowl she was sure his eyes would have been the same as Trevor's.

It made her tremble. He was hungry. And looking straight at her.

The man was striding toward her, his gait confident, purpose written on his face. Mary was suddenly shy and nervous. Her heart beat a fast tattoo and her breathing stuttered. She wasn't ready to meet him like this. Sure, she had things to tell him, but at the moment he looked as if he wanted to devour her. But what should she do?

His burning eyes made the decision for her. "Well, if he wants to pursue, I suppose this is as good a time as any to let him pursue," she murmured.

"Huh?" Holly said

"Ah, nothing," Mary replied just before hurrying off. Her hope was to blend in with the crowd of people standing and milling after the parade. Unfortunately, all that seemed to do was to slow her down. She looked over her shoulder and saw him, his eyes glued on her, ignoring comments from those passing by him.

Mary swallowed hard and headed down the street, directly behind the Santa sleigh. He was getting closer. The only thing she could do was to . . . join the parade. Surely he wouldn't follow her.

She made her way to the front of the float and thinking she'd lose him, she stepped in between the reindeer, ducking down.

"Mary? Whatcha doing?" Holly asked, giggling from the side.

Mary looked over to see Holly and a few of her friends following the parade, thinking she was participating in some kind of game. Great.

"Is something wrong down there?" Big Jed asked from his high perch. "One of the reindeer lose something?"

"No. Everything's fine. Get back to 'ho, ho, hoing,'" she said, peeking through the plastic animals. She grabbed sunglasses from one of the reindeer and donned the Orlando Magic baseball cap, keeping her head level with the reindeer. Surely he wouldn't follow her.

She'd miscalculated Trevor's resolve, as he continued to stride toward her. She rushed through the reindeer and bumped into a clarinet player from the jazz band. With a thud she bounced off his large ornament costume and nearly fell.

Continuing forward, she jogged past Santa's workshop, to the front of the float for her real estate company. She hopped on board and tried to open the door of the little house.

Ellen and Mayor Scott, who were walking alongside the float while Brad drove the truck pulling the float, surveyed Mary, wearing sunglasses and a baseball cap. "Mary, honey? Did you want something?" Ellen asked softly.

She continued to pull hard on the doorknob. "All . . . I . . . need . . . is to get inside." Huffing and puffing she said, "What's the deal, is it locked?"

"It's not a real house, Mary," the mayor said gently. "It's just a prop. There's no inside."

"Shoot!" She glanced around the float and saw Trevor still following.

"This is fun, Mary! How do we play?" Holly yelled.

Mary looked to see that Holly's little band of friends had grown to include teenagers and a few adults. "Holly. Go home. It's not a game." But the sounds of the parade drowned out her voice.

Without an explanation to Ellen or Howard, she jumped down and pushed her way through the Garden Club elves. All smiles, one of the members gave her a small poinsettia plant from the ones they were handing out to the crowd.

"Oh, no, thanks really," Mary muttered.

"Merry Christmas, dear," the elderly woman said and then went to get another plant.

Mary rushed forward toward the Nativity but decided against interfering with that float. The marching band was doing an intricate side step as she lumbered into their midst, trying not to get hit by drumsticks, trombones, and flags. Going past the Rotary float, a few of the members draped a red bow over her head but Mary was too busy trying to see where Trevor was to notice.

The church choral group was next. Mary smiled. Surely Trevor wouldn't be brazen enough to invade a sea of church parishioners in robes singing "Joy to the World." She carefully made her way into the middle of the group, still sporting the ball cap, sunglasses, red bow, carrying a poinsettia, and began to sing. She let out a sigh, deciding that she was probably safe from Tyrannosaurus Trevor.

A loud "Pardon me, excuse me" had her head jerking back. He was still coming! What had gotten into the man?

She scurried out of the group and past the cable company float, still working on their electronics. She weaved through the Senior Santas hoping to cut through an alley that was coming up. While she studied her escape route, one of the men took off his beard and draped it on her, causing the group to laugh.

Mary didn't notice. When she approached the alley she ran for it, knowing it would take her to Main Street, where she could get her bearings back. She chanced a glance behind and saw that Trevor was right behind her. Drat!

Down the alley she saw a utility closet. She headed for it, knowing that with the events of the day Colin would need access to the closet so it should be unlocked. She prayed it was unlocked.

She jerked the door open and received the surprise of her life.

Chapter Eighteen

Mary could not believe her eyes.

"Mom? Dad? What are you . . . what's . . ." Mary could feel her face turning red as she tried to form a coherent word.

There in front of her were her parents, in the midst of a seriously passionate kiss. Frank had his hands wrapped like an octopus around Merrilyn, who wore a sky-blue silk dress. Merrilyn's hands were just as busy in Frank's tousled hair. They slowly ended the kiss and turned to see the intruder.

"Sweetheart," Merrilyn said with a happy smile on her face, then narrowed her eyes. Seeing the sunglasses, ball cap, white beard, the red bow, and the poinsettia, she added, "It is you, isn't it?"

"Looks like you're enjoying the parade. Good. You did a wonderful job," Frank said reaching for the doorknob.

"Mary, your father and I . . . well, we . . ."

"Let her figure it out, darlin.' See you later." He added with a grin and closed the door.

Mary stood there, frozen. She wasn't sure if she wanted to jump for joy or gouge her eyes out for what she'd seen. A voice behind her got her feet moving.

"Mary! I want a word with you!"

She turned to see Trevor coming into the alley. Mary was so frazzled the only thing she knew to do was to run, her shaky legs leading her to the end of the alley. She broke into a jog then, ignoring his protests. The alley led to the top of Main Street, where the skating rink stood. She edged around it, avoiding anyone who called out to her. Or laughed at her unusual costume.

The end of the parade was just coming around the loop at the top of Main Street, where there was a small park with the town's Christmas tree and a beautiful fountain. She headed in that direction and saw that if she timed it just right, she could cross in front of the reindeers and make it to the park. Causing Trevor to be left on the other side, waiting for the reindeer and Santa's sleigh to pass.

She watched for her opening, her heart pounding in her chest, knowing Trevor was approaching. Just before the plastic animals crossed, she sprinted, jumping over the cable connection with the red SUV. She was so proud of herself she smiled, taking a deep breath to calm herself.

Then she heard the crowd gasp.

They were all gaping at something behind her, so she turned to see what it was.

Trevor had also managed to beat the reindeer. The crowd cheered loudly, not for Santa, but for Trevor's impressive athletic ability. Even

Big Jed stopped "Ho, ho, hoing" to give him a round of applause.

But Trevor's momentum from his amazing leap continued to carry him forward, into Mary, and unfortunately for her, straight for the fountain.

Trevor tried to grab her arm, her waist, her leg, but he couldn't get a solid grasp. She went over the edge and landed in the center of the Charity Memorial Fountain.

She sputtered as she sat in the water, pushing her wet hair out of her eyes. The sunglasses were askew and the now wet beard was drooping off her face. The red bow was drenched. But she still held the poinsettia in her hands. The crowd, including Holly and her posse, thought it was all part of the show and cheered, clapping wildly.

"You okay?" Trevor asked, standing next to the fountain.

She blew out a mouthful of fountain water. "Yeah. Sure. I always figured you'd get me back for pushing you into the pool."

With a wide grin, Trevor stepped over the ledge of the fountain and went to her. He reached down and took the plant from her. And the sunglasses, the ball cap, the beard, and the red bow and set them on the edge of the fountain. Then he pulled Mary up, keeping his arms around her holding her so close, his face was a breath away from hers. "Are you ready to listen to me now?"

His eyes had changed. The predator might have been lurking in the back, but now Mary saw softness, tenderness. Love. Her hands slid slowly up to his shoulders and said, "I'm listening."

"Mary Swenson, when I first met you, I thought you were an uptight, bossy, cold woman." Mary frowned at that. "But I couldn't have been more wrong. You're not only beautiful but warm, kind, and smart. I can't imagine my life without you."

Trevor whispered in her ear, "Honey, no job is worth losing you over. You take your mother's position; I'll find something else. I just want to be with you. I love you."

Mary lowered her head to his shoulder. "Really? Oh Trevor, I love you too. You make me a better person. And I can't imagine my life without you."

"Marry me."

Their eyes met and held.

"Well, son, you gonna kiss her or not?"

They turned to see that the Santa Sleigh had stopped in front of the fountain. Apparently Big Jed had signaled to Little Jed in the SUV to halt so he could watch the scene between them play out.

The crowd also was quiet waiting to see what would happen next.

"Just as soon as she gives me her answer, Santa," Trevor said. "Well, how about it, Mary with an 'a' one 'r'?"

She grinned and said, "Truce on pushing each other in any body of water?"

"For now," he teased.

She nodded and said, "Then yes."

Trevor gave an out of character whoop and kissed Mary passionately, causing everyone to whistle and cheer.

But Mary didn't care. She was in Trevor's arms. To stay.

The two couples snuggled in front of a roaring fire that night with glasses of celebratory champagne. Frank and Merrilyn were back together. They'd spent all afternoon . . . talking. They were going to make their marriage work this time.

Mary and Trevor had been busy also. After cleaning up after the parade, they went shopping for an engagement ring. She held her hand up, letting the engagement ring sparkle in the light of the fire as Trevor kissed her cheek.

"Trevor, dear, that's a beautiful ring. I think you both have excellent taste."

Mary snuggled closer to her fiancé. "I quite agree with you, Mom."

"You really think you're good enough for my daughter?" Frank asked, a twinkle in his eye.

"I know I'm not. But I'll do my best to make her happy every day of my life," Trevor replied.

Frank thought about that and said, "Good answer."

"Darling, now don't needle the boy. After all, look whom he's getting for in-laws. I wouldn't wish that on anyone." The four chuckled.

"So, Mom. You're moving back permanently?"

"Yes, I am. To be with your father." Merrilyn gave her husband a warm kiss. "I'm so glad that you asked me to come and help you with the parade, Mary."

Mary set down her drink and faced her mother confused. "I asked you?"

"Of course. I received a letter from you saying that you needed my help and would . . . I . . . assist you. You didn't write me for help?"

"No, Mom, I didn't."

"Well then who could have . . ." A beaming smile from Frank had Merrilyn playfully elbowing him in the stomach. "Frank! It was you, you sent that letter."

"I sure did. How else was I going to get my stubborn wife back to hash things out between us?"

Merrilyn sighed dreamily. "You did pursue me after all. Oh, my darling, I love you so much." She started dropping kisses all over her husband's face until he took control with his own steamy kiss.

"Okay. Offspring present. That's enough, you two," Mary said chuckling.

Merrilyn snuggled back against her husband. "I'm so happy to be back in Charity. I think I'm leaving Kennedy Swenson Events in good hands," she added with a wink to Mary.

"I think so too. I'll probably stay an assistant until the first child comes. Then I'd like to—"

"An assistant?" Trevor said. "What are you talking about?"

Mary turned to face him. "Sweetheart, Mom and I want the best person for the job of president of Kennedy Swenson Events. And that's you."

"What? You mean that . . . I'm . . . I'm going to . . ." Trevor couldn't seem to finish a sentence.

"Yes, and I'm going to take over Swenson Realty here in town." Her voice serious, Merrilyn said, "You've earned it, Trevor. No one knows the business better than you. Mary reminded me of that when she turned down the position."

"Although I think assistant could work. Don't you?" Mary asked, her brows lifting in question.

He gently took her hand and brought it to his lips for a kiss. "When do we start?" he said quietly.

It was quiet as both couples held each other. A group of carolers strolled by outside, singing of peace on earth, goodwill to all men.

Mary sighed pleasantly, finally feeling that wonderful Christmas sentiment. And she was very glad she hadn't gone to Bermuda for Christmas.

This Christmas had been a time of misunderstandings come to light, both the bad and the good. But more, a time for love, a time for forgiveness, and a time for miracles.

In other words, it had been an ordinary Christmas in the little town of Charity.

THE END

Thank you for reading *Merry Mary*.
Please take a moment to leave a review.
It helps authors so very much.
Thanks!!

Want more "Christmas in Charity"?
Keep reading for an excerpt of *Carol of the Bells*,
the next installment in the series.

Carol of the Bells

Chapter One

Carol Baker was in love. Unfortunately, the object of her affection had no idea that she actually existed.

As she walked along the main street of the little town of Charity, Florida, watching families and couples delighting in each other, she sighed for a brief second, indulging herself in all the what-ifs and if-onlys of life. What would it feel like to be there with someone? To walk arm-in-arm with the person you loved. And that loved you.

She knew her own attributes—pleasant, but plain face. Short reddish blonde hair, straight as a board. Her eyes were a muddy green, nothing to write sonnets about. And her occupation was absolutely nothing that any man would want to spend hours discussing. But she loved her job and wouldn't apologize for it. In her own small way, she was making a difference in the world. That was what was important.

Which brought her back to the reason why she was walking down the main street during the annual town's decorating party. Usually she just stayed home in her small apartment since she didn't like big crowds. Adult crowds, that is. But she knew he'd be here and she'd determined she'd seek him out to ask for his help with a project he'd hopefully be interested in. It wouldn't mean a thing, other than she'd be able to spend a little time with him. At least he'd learn her name, that was something.

She looked at the large twenty-foot tree standing at the top of the street. The cherry picker was in front with a lone figure at the top adding ornaments. Carol took a moment to appreciate. He was tall, much taller than she. His body was lanky without being awkward. As he reached for another ornament, he pushed up the black-rimmed glasses on his nose, a habit that made Carol smile. Her heart began a heavy pounding as she took a breath and walked to the tree.

"Hi, Miss Baker!"

Carol turned to see ten-year old Holly Jackson running up to her. A smile covered her face as she gave the young girl a hug. "Holly. How was your Thanksgiving, sweetheart?"

"It was crazy! Noel and I helped *Belle-mere* and Dad take care of the twins. Noel could even get them to smile. I got a laugh out of them once."

Carol chuckled. She was so happy for Holly's family. Her widowed father had fallen in love with Joy, a waitress from Hal's Place, the local diner, two years ago and everyone was thrilled when they had married. Four months ago, Joy had given birth to twin boys. Carol had taken gifts over to the family and had enjoyed holding the babies.

"I know that your stepmother is thankful to have you home from school so you can help."

"Yeah. But it's exhausting. I'll need to go back to school to rest up! Are you here to help decorate? I'm going down to Hal's Place to help Miss Grace."

"Oh yes, I'd heard she and Mac returned from their big trip."

"Yep. They're going to have a big party at their house to show some of the pictures they took traveling around the country."

"Well, that sounds wonderful." Mac was a world-famous photographer whose pictures were pieces of Americana. She couldn't wait to see his new shots of America through the four seasons of a year.

Holly waved goodbye and headed in the opposite direction. Carol looked back to the town's tree, straightened her shoulders, and trudged forward. She was going to do this if it killed her. The way her heart was pounding in her chest, it just might.

The tree was stunning, with large brightly colored balls, gingerbread men, stars, and bells. That reminded her. She needed to check in at the Presbyterian Church for the new schedule of practice for the Christmas concert.

Sweat formed on her brow and her throat tightened while she waited. With a deep breath she gave herself another pep talk, again running through her mind just the right words to say. She'd rehearsed them over and over, not wanting to come off looking like a fool. When the cherry picker started to make its way down, her breath caught in her throat and her heartbeat doubled. It was time.

After swallowing hard, she approached the man. Her mouth opened to speak but before anything came out, Mayor Howard Scott moved in.

"Great job, Brad," he said shaking the man's hand. "Looks wonderful. You want to get to the switch and be ready to turn this thing on when I give you the signal."

"Sure, Howard."

Brad walked back behind the small stage before Carol could get her tongue to work. Just as well. He'd be distracted and she needed his full attention.

She stood back with the others as the mayor took the stage and, standing before a microphone, welcomed everyone for the lighting of the town's tree. They had a brief countdown and when the tree lit up, everyone "oohed" and "aahed" over the bright glow of brilliant lights, the shimmering ornaments and festive colors. Carol couldn't help being drawn into the excitement.

Then she saw Brad make his way from behind the stage, glancing up at the tree, probably inspecting it for any problems. Carol took a breath and started toward him.

But music came on the loudspeakers along with a narration about the town of Charity. Carol closed her eyes and winced, knowing that her opportunity had passed for another fifteen minutes at least.

She knew what the music and narration signaled—the Florida snow that was a trademark of their little town. It was the first "snow" of the season, actually soap flakes and bubbles that would stream from boxes attached to the lampposts. Everyone always went crazy over it. Originally from Ohio, she thought it a bit silly.

Just as predicted, when the snow started, everyone cheered and went out onto Main Street to catch flakes and take pictures. Carol shook her head and turned to find Brad, but somehow the man had disappeared.

"No, no, no!" She'd built up her courage, she'd practiced her lines. She was ready now to speak with him. No snowstorm was going to stop her. Her eyes scanned the area, determined to find him.

And there he was, in the middle of the street, snow falling all around him, talking with Mary and Trevor Crane. Carol's first inclination was to tense up, since Brad and Mary had dated at one time. But that was before Mary and Trevor had fallen in love. They must have come to town for Thanksgiving weekend.

She liked Mary. Especially since Mary had always noticed her and been kind to her. But secretly she couldn't have been happier when Trevor had come along and stolen Mary from Brad.

Carefully, Carol made her way toward them, dodging excited kids, their parents chasing them, and the tourists that were still marveling at the event. Just before she reached her target, Mary kissed Brad on the cheek, Trevor shook his hand, and the two walked away, hand-in-hand. Carol sighed at the romantic gesture.

His back to her, she stopped a couple of feet from Brad and took another deep breath. Before she could utter a syllable, he turned and saw her standing there. A grin filled his face, his brown eyes dancing behind his glasses. "Hello."

Carol was melting quicker than the soap bubbles. The sounds of applause, laughter, and camera shutters all meshed together into mindless noise as she stared at him. "Ah . . ." Every brilliant opening sentence flew from her brain. She stood there frozen, muttering, "Ah."

His grin widened and his eyes went back to the snow as he said, "It's a nice night, isn't it?"

"Ah, I'm Carol." *Brilliant. Great opening line.*

Brad gave a slight chuckle, sticking his hands in his pockets as his gaze returned to her. "I know who you are, Carol," he said, his voice a low murmur.

That nearly floored her. *Dr. Bradley Moore, famous scientist, professor at the university, knows my name?*

"How are you?" he asked casually.

His brown eyes appeared as yummy chocolate balls. She could imagine herself falling into them. But he'd asked her a question, didn't he? She straightened her shoulders trying to compose herself. "I'm fine. The, ah, tree looks great."

Brad glanced in that direction, the lights reflected in his eyes. "Yeah, it does." He cocked his head to the side, considering. "Could probably use a few more colored balls at the top. You know, to be more symmetrical."

"I think you did a wonderful job," she crooned and when he again smiled at her, she cleared her throat and decided to get to the business at hand.

"I was wondering if you had a few free minutes to discuss a . . . something that I . . . I, ah, I'd like to proposition you." Her eyes widened with horror. Did she really just say that? Of all the stupid things.

Apparently Brad wasn't phased but only chuckled. "Okay, that sounds interesting."

"I'm sorry. That didn't come out right. What I meant to say was that I . . . I need you." She could feel her face go red. Could she be any more verbally clumsy? She did know how to speak with human beings, didn't she? "And why don't I just stop talking now before you think I'm a total moron."

"Why would I think that?" His simple answer took her by surprise. "You obviously have something important to talk to me about. Look, I can't talk now but how about we meet. Maybe tomorrow? Hal's Place?"

Hope blossomed in her chest. She smiled slightly and said, "What time?"

He narrowed his eyes and she noticed the cutest crinkling at the edges. Sheesh, she was really going to have to get a grip. "I've got another meeting there at five so how about we say four thirty. That give you enough time?"

Her heart lightened. It was perfect. And she'd have another day to perfect her pitch. "Yes.

That would work. Thank you so much," she said, her smile widening.

He returned the smile. "You're very welcome. Carol."

"All right, you two. Give me a smile."

They both looked over to see Mac aiming a camera at them. Brad didn't hesitate but moved closer to Carol and put his arm around her. She fought the shiver that wanted to spread from the simple touch and tried to just enjoy the moment.

"Great. Thanks. Tree looks awesome as usual, Brad," Mac said before quickly moving on to get other snapshots of the evening.

Brad dropped his arm and said, "So I'll see you tomorrow then, at Hal's?"

"I'll be there."

She practically skipped home, proud of herself for confronting her fears and talking to Brad Moore—the man of her dreams.

But that fact would have to be put away for now. There was a more important issue on the table and she needed Brad. He could mean the difference between success and failure. She'd work all night if she had to, polishing up her presentation. He just had to say yes.

Not for her, but for the kids. Yeah, that was the ticket. That would be her compelling argument. And if he were half the man she thought he was, he'd surely agree. She sighed.

And if the thought of deep brown eyes were a part of that sigh, well, there was nothing wrong with that, was there?

Get your copy of *Carol of the Bells*,
Available at online bookstores.

Your free books are waiting!

Do you enjoy sweet romance, holiday stories, Christian Fiction?

You can get three stories for free. That's right, three! It's a special gift to you for signing up for Malinda Martin's monthly newsletter.

To get your free books, go to www.malindamartin.com. You'll also receive information on other sweet romance and Christian fiction novels.

Enjoy the season with these "Christmas In Charity" titles:

Christmas Grace

It's the most wonderful time of the year for everyone in Charity except Grace Hudson. She associates Christmas with bad memories and is determined to be immune from the cheerful holiday. All she really wants is to sell the diner that she inherited and move far away. Award-winning photographer Stuart "Mac" McCrae needs to get that one perfect picture before heading south for the holidays. The only thing holding him back is the small, undecorated diner that sits in the middle of the beautiful main street of Charity. Book one in the series.

Comfort And Joy

Joy Bisset never lives anywhere for long. However, Charity, Florida is slowly capturing her heart. And seeing Holly, Noel, and their lonely father Ross struggling, she can't help but lend a hand.

Ross Jackson is swamped, running a business and raising his two children. So the lonely widower can't resist the offer from the petite new waitress at Hal's Place to help with the kids.

Then when Joy needs help, Ross and his family come to her rescue. It doesn't have to be personal and he doesn't have to forget the vows he made to his late wife. And she doesn't have to lose her heart to the strong, handsome man. But Christmas is a season for miracles, especially in Charity.

Merry Mary

All your favorite Charity characters are back to enjoy the season in the charming small town that lives up to its name. Mary Swenson's vision of a quiet Christmas spent with her father is shattered when she's made the director of the Charity, Florida Christmas Eve Parade. Then her estranged mother, a successful events planner in New York, shows up with a sexy assistant to help plan the parade.

Trevor Crane isn't exactly sure why he's in a small Florida town for the holidays. He only knows that his employer, the spirited Merrilyn Kennedy Swenson, needs him and if he's going to take over her business one day, he'll do her bidding. Even if it means ignoring her beautiful daughter.

Carol of the Bells

It's Christmas in Charity, which means time for another sweet Christmas romance. Shy, kindergarten teacher Carol Baker is in love with the resident scientist slash professor. Problem is he doesn't know her. Dr. Bradley Moore is making a splash in the science world but finds himself distracted when the pretty teacher asks for his assistance with a project. With counsel and help (?) from Grace, Big Jed, Holly, and others in Charity, maybe this unlikely pair will get together. But not before they learn the true meaning of the words of the Christmas angel—"Fear not."

Faith, Hope, & Mistletoe

Widowed mom Faith Hamilton can't seem to earn enough money for her family this Christmas. When her friend, single dad Marcus Carrington, needs her help and suggests a profitable collaboration, she wonders if she's foolish for agreeing. Especially since she's starting to have feelings for the man.

Goode Tidings

Take a trip to small town America for another sweet holiday romance in Charity, Florida.

Cynical reporter Jill Goode is on assignment in Charity. And to visit the mother she tries to avoid. Andy Montgomery, a successful baker from New York, is home in Charity for the holidays. Both find things different than what they expected and will need each other, as well as the love of Charity, to overcome the problems facing them for the holidays.

Available at online bookstores.

For more romantic holiday stories, check out these books:

Sleep In Heavenly Peace Inn

Three couples at the Sleep in Heavenly Peace Inn must deal with their tumultuous relationships. With the help of three children, a man with a white beard, the inn's mysterious manager, and a reindeer, maybe they can do just that.

Christmas Dad

Bethany and Samuel Fitzgerald are tired of having no dad for the holidays. When they discover a friendly transient at the inner city help center where their mother volunteers, they devise a plan to hire him to be their "Christmas Dad."

Forgetting Christmas

Ali Benson wakes up from a car crash with the last six months of her life forgotten. Along with the fact that she's engaged to marry Michael Grayson, her handsome boss, on Christmas Day. Ali and Michael deal with the season in different ways as she tries to remember and he tries to forget. But this Christmas they'll both have to confront the truth. And hopefully find that sometimes remembering is the best part of Christmas.

Available at online bookstores.

Dear Reader,

I hope you enjoyed another visit to Charity, Florida. How did you like the Christmas Eve parade? That was so much fun to write.

I always love writing stories set in Charity. Its charm and warmth are what we all wish for in a small town, in our own Christmas celebration. Hopefully, *Merry Mary* filled you with Christmas cheer and gave you a chuckle or two.

The inspiration for Frank and Merrilyn came from an old movie, *McLintock!* that starred John Wayne and Maureen O'Hara. Check it out sometime. You'll see where I got the idea for the chase at the end.

Your thoughts and encouragement mean the world to me. You can reach me at malindamartinbooks@gmail.com. And if you like *Merry Mary* please be sure to post a review.

It's my hope that the true spirit of the season will rest with you and your family. May it be your best Christmas ever!

Blessings,
M.M.

Made in the USA
Columbia, SC
15 January 2024

30488504R00143